A Study of Contemporary Henan Urban Literature and Urban Image

Authored by Wei Huaying

Translated by Lu Zhiguo（陆志国）

CHICAGO ACADEMIC PRESS

A Study of Contemporary Henan Urban Literature and Urban Image
Authored by Wei Huaying
Translated by Lu Zhiguo（陆志国）
Language: English
Word Count (for space of all pages): Approximately 160,000 words
Publisher: Chicago Academic Press
Number of Pages: 244
ISBN: 978-1-965890-92-9

Publishing	Chicago Academic Press
	5923 N Artesian Ave
	Chicago IL 60659
Email	contact@chicagoacademicpress.com
Website	http://chicagoacademicpress.com/
Book Size	6X9 inches
First Edition	November, 2025

CONTENT

Introduction

With the acceleration of urbanization, urban literature has proliferated and garnered increasing scholarly attention. According to incomplete statistics, since 2011, urban themes have accounted for over half of short stories, while a significant number of novels have emerged that depict urban life. Poetry and prose, too, strive to capture urban experiences and the spirit of the city. In contrast, rural literature has shown signs of "fatigue" in its confrontation with the robust rise of urban narratives. It is evident that urban literature has become an inescapable topic in the new century and will undoubtedly remain a vital branch of future literature. As urbanization progresses, urban literature is increasingly intertwined with the lived realities of contemporary Chinese society and its developmental trajectory. As Jin Yucheng, author of *Blossoms*, remarked in an interview with *China Reading Weekly*, "Chinese literature will soon fully shift to urban narratives."[①] Such creative trends suggest that the future quality of Chinese literature may well depend on the caliber of its urban literary production.

The growth of cities and the surge in urban literature have spurred widespread academic interest in the field. This burgeoning focus intersects with the emergence of post-70s and post-80s writers, as well as the broader call

① Jin Yucheng: "Chinese Literature Will Soon Fully Shift to Urban Narratives," China Reading Weekly, October 31, 2018.

for literature to "engage with reality and document the present." The study of urban literature has thus become a critical lens through which to understand contemporary literary creation. Internationally, research on urban literature and urban studies has been underway for decades, offering valuable theoretical frameworks. In contrast, China's urban literary studies remain nascent, characterized by:

1. The absence of comprehensive monographs systematically examining contemporary urban literature;

2. A predominance of case studies and reactive criticism, rather than problematized or systematic analysis;

3. Imprecise grasp of urban culture, ethos, consciousness, and experiences reflected in the literature, hindering effective theoretical construction;

4. Overemphasis on Beijing, Shanghai, Xi'an, Guangzhou, and Shenzhen, with insufficient attention to the distinctiveness of other cities.

Henan's Urban Literature: Gaps and Potential

In the context of Henan, scholars have noted that since the 1990s, as urban literary output has expanded, more writers have turned their focus to cities and the interplay between urban spaces and their inhabitants. This includes both older writers' sensitivity to urban development and younger writers' enthusiasm for metropolitan life. Yet, as a province with deep rural traditions, Henan's literary discourse has prioritized pastoral and agrarian themes, leaving its urban narratives fragmented and understudied. The lack of systematic research has obscured the relationship between Henan's urban literature and its regional culture, while failing to integrate sociological, geographical, and urban studies perspectives. Consequently, Henan's urban literary identity—whether in terms of its subjects, character, or the distinctiveness of its cities—remains nebulous, demanding scholarly resolution.

Regional Specificity and Civilizational Legacy

Examining the "city in literature" through a regional lens reveals the diversity and complexity of China's urban cultural identity. Henan, as a cradle of Chinese civilization with a luminous historical legacy, also bears the marks of geographical constraints—manifested in traits like cultural conservatism. Within this framework, Henan's urban literature not only addresses universal urban themes but also grapples with unique regional questions: the weight of ancient capital cultures, distinctively Central Plains modes of social interaction and survival, and the psychological fissures wrought by modernization, demolition, and urban assimilation. Literature here transcends mere artistry; it actively mirrors—and intervenes in—social transformation and urban metamorphosis. In this sense, studying Henan's urban literature becomes a vital means to document, excavate, and even anticipate the evolution of urban culture.

The Rise of Henan's Urban Literature

Since the 1990s, urban literature has flourished in China, with Shanghai,

Beijing, Shenzhen, Xi'an, and Wuhan emerging as its primary hubs and narrative settings. As urbanization swept across the country, distinct urban cultures and literary traditions took root. Henan, though traditionally an agrarian stronghold, accelerated its urban transformation during the Reform and Opening era, giving rise to a corpus of locally grounded urban narratives that showcase unique metropolitan landscapes. Works such as Zhang Yigong's *The Distant Posthouse*, Li Peifu's *City White Paper*, *The City's Light*, *Waiting for the Soul*, and *The Book of Life*, Zhang Yu's *Soccer Gate* and *Weakness*, Shao Li's *My Quality of Life* and *Minghui's Christmas*, Qiao Ye's *I Truly Love You*, *Demolition Chronicles*, and *The Pearl Journal*, Chen Tiejun's *Old Miscellany*, Nan Feiyan's *Scorpio*, and Xi Tongfa's *Sparrow Dialogue* all reflect Henan's urban culture through a regional lens. These novels weave the province's history and contemporary realities into their narratives, using characters' emotional journeys to trace urban metamorphosis while interrogating collective memory and quotidian life in Henan's cities.

The "Urban Emotions" series by Yang Dongming, Du Lixin, and Sun Yu further documents the existential and affective states of city dwellers. Younger writers like Chen Hongwei, Li Qingyuan, Wang Xiaopeng, and essayist Yu He, attuned to urban rhythms, contribute fresh perspectives. Notably, the "Three Arts Collective" (He Hong, Feng Jie, Zhang Xiaolin) infuses their calligraphy, painting, and poetry with Zhongyuan cultural motifs. By mapping this literary terrain, we can delineate Henan's literary evolution—particularly its ideological shift from rural to urban paradigms since 1949—

while identifying individual divergences within this broader transition. Such an excavation not only reveals the interplay between Henan's urban literature and regional culture but also facilitates the construction of Henan's urban identity within China's national literary framework. Literary portrayals of Zhengzhou, Kaifeng, and Luoyang can amplify these cities' cultural resonance nationwide.

Methodology and Scholarly Interventions

This study adopts a diachronic approach to Henan's urban literary history, combining textual analysis with empirical research to assess its achievements and canonical status. It probes the genre's regional attributes, cultural psychology, and spiritual ethos, alongside emergent urban-literary dynamics. Post-1990s, Henan's urban narratives have gradually shed the dominance of rural writing, reclaiming discursive space and revitalizing China's premodern/modern tradition of civic literature. Through these texts, we trace how socialist legacies and historical sedimentation shape new aesthetic forms amid societal change.

Cities function not merely as habitats but as crucibles of civilization. The study prioritizes decoding urban semiotics—from Kaifeng's drum music and colonial-era architecture to Zhengzhou's Dehua Street and time-honored brands—where ancient heritage and modernity converge. Literary archetypes like "the migrant," "the outsider," and "the native" embody polyphonic urban identities, refracting the complexities of post-reform society through individual memories.

As polymorphic cultural spaces, cities demand pluralistic readings. Henan's urban literature serves as an archive of cultural transition: Chen Tiejun's *Old Miscellany* preserves vanishing folkways, while Qiao Ye's *The Pearl Journal* celebrates Henan's culinary heritage. Jiao Shu's *House Trilogy* and *Mayor Series* grapple with neoliberal anxieties. In our globalized, (post)modern era, these narratives gain urgency by resisting homogenization, capturing both urban materiality and the psychic tremors of its inhabitants.

Research Innovations and Limitations

Employing comparative literature and historical contextualization, this project pioneers systematic research on Henan's urban literature—a field hitherto overlooked. Through close reading and archival recovery, it reconstructs developmental trajectories while situating local expressions within national socio-literary currents. Though constrained by scope and the genre's inherent complexity, this work lays the groundwork for future scholarship at the intersection of urban studies, cultural geography, and literary historiography.

Chapter 1
Defining Urban Literature

Urban literature emerges as a cultural byproduct of urbanization. Lewis Mumford posits that Western cities originated first as sacred sites with religious significance, then evolved into agrarian villages focused on domestication, pottery, and land cultivation, before finally developing into politically fortified citadels.① In contrast, China's urban centers grew from the dual foundations of *cheng* (walled settlements for defense) and *shi* (commercial hubs for trade). The shi represents the earliest prototype of urbanity, fundamentally distinguished from rural settlements by its economic function.② "Over the past century and a half, urbanization has primarily been driven by economic growth and technological innovation, enabling mass production and concentrated labor forces. A large-scale factory implies a densely concentrated population society—it signifies, fundamentally, the migration of the labor force, and thus the total population, toward urban centers."③ The city, as an emblem of civilization, presents contemporary urban literature with numerous dilemmas in effectively responding to rapidly evolving social conditions—especially when contrasted with the flourishing tradition of classical Chinese urban writing. As noted in scholarly research, "From a literary-

① (US) Lewis Mumford: *The City in History: Its Origins, Its Transformations, and Its Prospects*, trans. Ni Wenyan and Song Junling, China Architecture & Building Press, 2008, pp. 1-26.

② Fu Chonglan, Bai Chenxi, et al.: *A History of Chinese Urban Development*, Social Sciences Academic Press, 2009, p. 35.

③ (U.S.) Simon Kuznets: *Economic Growth of Nations: Total Output and Production Structure*, trans. Chang Xun et al., The Commercial Press, 1985, p. 87.

historical perspective, while Balzac, Turgenev, and Tolstoy wrote during periods that predated their nations' industrial zenith, they nevertheless centered their works on urban life. By comparison, Chinese urban-themed literature remains far less developed than its rural counterpart."① A comparative analysis of urban narratives in classical and contemporary Chinese literature—while tracing the creative evolution of China's urban literary tradition—confronts the seminal question of literature's role in urban development.

1. The Conceptualization of Cities and Urban Literature

In ancient China, urban literature had always been the mainstream of literary tradition. As early as the pre-Qin and Han dynasties, the term "city"appeared in classical texts. *Han Feizi • Ai Chen* states: "Though a high-ranking minister may enjoy generous emoluments, he must not wield power in the city; though his faction may be numerous, he must not command soldiers." This might be the earliest recorded usage of "city" in Chinese classics.Moreover, in *Strategies of the Warring States: Zhao I - The King of Qin Speaks to Prince Ta*, there is an account of Feng Ting, the governor of Shangdang in the state of Han, secretly sending an envoy to petition the King of Zhao with these words: "We now possess seventy walled cities and settlements, which we humbly offer to Your Majesty. May Your Majesty deign to

① Chen Xihan: "Compared to the Flourishing of Rural Literature, Urban Literary Creation is Markedly Underdeveloped," Wenhui Daily, September 6, 2018, p. 7.

accept them." In Book of the Later Han: Biography of Liao Fu: "He habitually dwelled by his ancestors' graves, never once entering a walled market-city (chengshi)." Though the term "city" in that era could not carry the rich connotations it holds today, it already represented a conceptual fusion of "walled settlement" (cheng) and "marketplaces" (shi). Its emergence during the Warring States period was no coincidence—Chinese cities had developed significantly since the Spring and Autumn period, reaching considerable prosperity by the Warring States era.

From the Han dynasty onward, literary works increasingly depicted urban scenes, such as Ban Gu's *Ode to the Eastern Capital* and *Ode to the Western Capital*, alongside Zhang Heng's *Ode to the Western Capital* and *Ode to the Eastern Capital*, have documented the splendor of contemporary cities. Later, vernacular fiction from the Tang to the Qing dynasties—such as the bustling urban life in *Jin Ping Mei*, or *Dream of the Red Chamber* and *The Scholars* (hailed as "Southern Wu and Northern Cao shining together")—established urban literature as a distinct tradition. Republican-era fiction further enriched this tradition with vivid portrayals of Shanghai's cosmopolitan scenes, Beijing's ancient capital life, and the urban middle-class existence depicted by Shanghai-style writers, all contributing vibrant depictions of city life to literary history.

Following the establishment of the People's Republic, China's urban structure underwent significant transformation. By 1949, the country had only 69 designated cities, with urban dwellers comprising a mere 10.6% of the total population. Subsequently, influenced by prevailing ideology, cities were viewed as bourgeois enclaves, prompting their functional reorientation from consumption hubs to production centers. Consequently, for an extended period, the very concept of urbanity became a target of critique and transformation, resulting in literature's ambiguous stance toward cities. This ideological climate even led to the demonization of urban spaces in numerous literary and cinematic works—exemplified by the novel *Between Us, a Couple*, and films like *Sentinels Under the Neon Lights* and *Never Forget*, which polemically framed cities as bastions of materialism and bourgeois decadence. These ideological currents condemned both cities and urban literature to prolonged suppression and stagnation, creating a cultural environment where their development was systematically stifled.

In the post-reform era, China reopened its doors and embarked on modernization through reform and opening-up policies, breaking the long stagnation of urban development. In 1979, Wu Youren of Nanjing University broke theoretical barriers with his groundbreaking paper *On Socialist Urbanization in China*, which marked the formal beginning of domestic urbanization studies and accelerated the subsequent urbanization process. As scholar Cui Yuanmin observed: "Urbanization is a human-centered systemic transformation involving both hard infrastructure and soft institutional frameworks—a comprehensive shift from traditional to modern society."① The watershed moment came in 1984 when the Third Plenum of the 12th Central Committee passed *The Decision on Economic System Reform*, officially affirming cities as the nation's economic, political, scientific, and cultural hubs; concentrations of modern industry and the working class; leading forces in socialist modernization. The document declared: "Only through systematic reform can urban economies flourish, meet the demands of domestic revitalization and international openness, and truly fulfill their leading role in propelling national development." This policy not only rehabilitated cities ideologically but also launched China's unprecedented urban transformation.

Following this pivotal shift, China's urban development entered a period of rapid expansion. Sociological data reveals that between 1978 and 1993, the number of Chinese cities with populations exceeding 500,000 surged from 40 to 68. This urbanization trend accelerated notably after 1993—by 2000, the urban population ratio reached 36.22%, marking a 15-percentage-point increase from 1982 at the dawn of reform and opening-up. Metropolises like Shanghai, Beijing, and Tianjin had already surpassed global urbanization averages by this stage.② Entering the 21st century,

---

① Cui Yuanmin et al.: *Urbanization Strategies and Countermeasures in Hebei Province*, Hebei Science and Technology Press, 1998, p. 20.

② Hong Dayong: "Social Development and Consumption Diversification Since the Reform Era," in Media and Life: The Business Strategies of Lifestyle Newspapers and Magazines, edited by the Media Management Research Institute, Renmin University of

China's urbanization pace intensified further. By the end of 2016, the national urbanization rate stood at 57.4%, with projections indicating it would reach 60% by 2020. This underscores that in contemporary China, over half the population now resides in urban areas, their lives inextricably intertwined with cities. Literature, as a vital reflection of social life, must engage with this reality.

As urban development accelerates, the relationship between cities and literature has remained a focal point of academic inquiry. The perennial question—"What is a city?"—has spurred the translation and introduction of seminal Western urban theories into Chinese scholarship, including Max Weber and Georg Simmel's sociological frameworks, Jürgen Habermas' concept of the urban public sphere, and Walter Benjamin's cultural theories. Benjamin's *The Arcades Project and The Work of Art in the Age of Mechanical Reproduction*, which explore the poet's relationship with urban modernity, have been particularly influential. Additionally, seminal theoretical works include American scholar Burton Pike' s The Image of the City in Modern Literature, which *"traces the contours of urban representation—from early myths, epics, and biblical narratives to 19th- and 20th-century literary works"* in the European tradition,① and Richard Lehan's *The City in Literature* (Chinese edition, Shanghai People's Publishing House, 2009), which examines how

China, Xinhua Publishing House, 2003, p. 12.

① Chen Xiaolan: *Paris and Shanghai in Literature: A Study of Zola and Mao Dun*, Guangxi Normal University Press, 2006, p. 7.

literary depictions of cities evolve alongside historical and cultural transformations. Lehan offers a pivotal insight: "When oral communication fails—when elders cannot transmit knowledge beyond their lifespan—cities demand writing systems. As Lewis Mumford observed, cities emerged historically through 'permanent written forms and symbols (*The City in History*, p.97)."①

These studies emphasize the sociological and geographical significance of cities. "The city is a geographical marker of modern society, a milestone in the process of social modernization."② "It is simultaneously a landscape, an economic space, a population density, a hub of life and labor—or, put differently, "a kind of atmosphere, a character, or even a soul."③ As Mike Crang posits, "Fiction may contain deeper insights into urbanity. We must not reduce it to mere documentation of city life while neglecting its revelatory power. The city is not merely a backdrop for narratives—depictions of its geographical landscapes equally articulate understandings of society and lived experience. ... Thus, the imperative lies not in realistic portrayals of cities or urban existence, but in interpreting the meaning of urban spaces and cityscapes."④

---

① (U.S.) Richard Lehan: *The City in Literature: An Intellectual and Cultural History*, Shanghai People's Publishing House, 2009, p. 15.

② Luo Qianglie: "*Three Essays on Literature,*" Tianjin Literature, no. 12, 1987.

③ Liu Lequn: "The Contemporary Urban Ecological Mentality and Artistic Creation Project," Tianjin Literature, no. 9, 1987.

④ (UK) Mike Crang: *Cultural Geography*, Nanjing University Press, 2005, p. 50.

American scholar Rhoads Murphey, in his 1953 book *Shanghai: Key to Modern China*, which examines Shanghai's history from 1843 to 1949, posits that "Shanghai, along with the patterns of its growth and development over the past century, has always been a microcosm of modern China." He contends that "Shanghai provides the key to understanding what has already happened—and what will happen—in modern China," offering both a fresh perspective and a method of interpretation.

Since the turn of the new century, the translation and introduction of Western urban cultural studies has accelerated significantly. Bao Yaming spearheaded this movement by editing influential series such as Modernity and the Production of Space, Postmetropolis and Cultural Studies, and Critical Studies of Postmetropolis Cities and Regions, which brought Henri Lefebvre, Edward Soja, and other theorists' urban cultural theories to Chinese academia. Wang Min'an and Chen Yongguo co-edited *The Urban Culture Reader*, providing comprehensive coverage of Western urban cultural research. Guangxi Normal University Press published Xue Yi's four-volume *Readings in Western Urban Cultural Studies*, while Leo Ou-fan Lee's *Shanghai Modern: The Flowering of a New Urban Culture in China* (2001) ignited a wave of scholarship on Shanghai's urban culture. These works collectively shifted scholarly focus toward examining the intertextual relationship between cities and literature.

The translation and publication of these theoretical works injected fresh perspectives and methodologies into domestic research. Contemporary Chinese urban literature, long suppressed after the establishment of worker-peasant-soldier literary traditions, experienced its revival only in the post-reform era. A pivotal moment came in 1983 when academia convened the first "Urban Literature Theory Conference" in Beidaihe. The following year saw the launch of Urban Literature magazine in Taiyuan, Shanxi, which in 1988 dedicated a special column to conceptualizing "urban literature," featuring prominent critic Zhang Jiong's seminal essay Random Thoughts on "Urban Literature." Concurrently, literary journals like Guangzhou Literature and Shanghai Literature began documenting the gradual shift in literary focus from rural to urban themes during China's social transformation. This period marked the beginning of sustained academic attention to the intricate relationship between urban culture and urban fiction.

Zhao Yuan's *Beijing: The City and Its People* (published by Shanghai People's Publishing House in 1991) stands as China's earliest scholarly work examining "the city in literature." This pioneering study, followed by deepening research on the Beijing School and Shanghai School of literature, established "the literary city" as a transformative conceptual framework that expanded academic horizons. The late 1990s witnessed a cultural resurgence of urban memory through Jiangsu Fine Arts Publishing House's nostalgic photo collections like Old Beijing, Old Suzhou, and Old Guangzhou. Institutional recognition followed with Shanghai Normal University establishing its Urban Culture Research Center in 1998, attracting scholars including Sun

Xun, Bao Yaming, and Jiang Jian from Shanghai, alongside Tao Dongfeng, Jin Yuanpu, Wang Min'an, and Luo Gang from Beijing.

The influx of domestic and international theories complicated attempts to define urban literature, spawning competing terms like "metropolitan literature" and "street-life literature" that created conceptual ambiguity. Professor Chen Xiaoming articulated a precise framework, arguing that while contemporary Chinese literature's greatest achievements—works of global significance—have overwhelmingly focused on rural narratives, this represents a paradox for an era of rapid urbanization and globalization. He proposed three essential criteria for authentic urban literature:

1. Geographical Specificity

Works must depict concrete urban environments and lifestyles

2. Urban Consciousness

Texts must demonstrate awareness of urban existence—where characters or narrators consciously grapple with their metropolitan condition. This often manifests as modernist or postmodernist self-awareness.

3. Formal Innovation

The narrative style or poetic language must evolve in dialogue with urban experience

In essence, Chen defines urban literature as works that "portray city life while embodying urban consciousness." His taxonomy provides crucial scaffolding for analyzing China's evolving literary engagement with urbanization.

This conceptual framework carries particular weight because earlier scholarship had left urban literature in a state of theoretical ambiguity, often conflating it with "metropolitan literature" and creating persistent definitional challenges. Leading scholars have since advanced nuanced interpretations that collectively clarify the field's contours. Chen Pingyuan posits that cities function as vital ecosystems for literary creation and circulation, arguing that "it is precisely through this cultural transmission that cities gain meaning—without literature, urban spaces risk becoming sterile concrete jungles reduced to commutes, subways, and shopping malls."[①] Bai Ye offers a complementary definition by framing metropolitan literature as "contemporary writing that takes modern cities as its stage to document urban living, forge new civic identities, and excavate the distinctive emotional cadences of metropolitan existence."

These interventions collectively reposition urban literature studies to address pressing questions: how literary texts metabolize the material realities of cities, whether urban writing demands unique aesthetic innovations, and to what extent urbanity has supplanted rurality as China's dominant literary

① Chen Pingyuan: "*The Possibility of Urban Literary Studies*," Lecture at East China Normal University. March 16, 2011. https://www.doc88.com/p-9445405560378.html.

imaginary. The evolving discourse now moves beyond definitional debates to examine literature's role in shaping—and being shaped by—China's unfolding urban revolution.

However, some scholars argue that these concepts should still be treated as distinct subjects requiring careful differentiation. Zhang Guangming points out that there are inherent differences between "metropolitan literature" and "urban literature". "The term 'metropolis' specifically refers to large cities or cosmopolitan hubs, while 'city' encompasses a much broader scope, including not only major urban centers but also emerging mid-sized and small cities." Consequently, the concept of "metropolitan literature" is narrower in coverage compared to "urban literature.""Metropolitan literature" emphasizes the distinct flavor, sensibility, mindset, and spirit of big cities—focusing more on depicting the cultural traditions and contemporary realities of urban life. In contrast, "urban literature" highlights the political, economic, and cultural totality of cities, delving deeper into the relationship between cities and their inhabitants, as well as the interplay between urbanization and human transformation. Zhao Yanqiu shares a similar view, arguing that only works depicting metropolitan life—particularly lifestyles unique to large cities and distinct from those of smaller towns or rural areas—can be considered true "metropolitan literature." From today's perspective, the term "metropolis" would thus be limited to megacities like Beijing, Shanghai, and Guangzhou. Yet many scholars also recognize that, despite Chinese writers having incorporated cities and urbanization into their artistic vision early on, urban literature has historically lagged behind rural literature in both scale and literary achievement within the binary framework of urban-rural literary traditions. This disparity is evident in the dominance of rural themes among award-winning works and the oeuvres of celebrated contemporary authors. However, this trend has begun to shift in recent years. Works like *Song of Everlasting Sorrow* and *Blossoms*, which center on urban life, have won the Mao Dun Literary Prize, while the rise of "post-70s" and "post-80s" writers—who draw from their own urban experiences—has enriched the diversity of urban literary expression.

2. Regional Writing and Urban Imagination

The resurgence of Chinese urban literature since the 1980s began with works deeply rooted in regional identity. In 1980, Lu Wenfu pioneered his "Chronicles of Alleyway Dwellers" series. Having lived long-term in Suzhou, the author captured its distinctive social customs and humanistic textures with remarkable artistic specificity. Similarly, Fan Xiaoqing's *The Romance of Pants Alley* vividly portrays the joys and sorrows of Suzhou's alleyway residents. Beginning in 1980, Chen Jiangong authored a series of Beijing-themed novels including *There's a Rascal in West Beijing*, *Phoenix Eyes*, and *No. 9, Huluba Hutong*. In 1985, Deng Youmei published *Inside and Outside the Capital*, dedicated to depicting Beijing's urban life. Subsequent works like *Tales of Taoranting*, *In Search of Painter Han*, *That Fifth*, and *Snuff Bottles* collectively crafted quintessentially Beijing characters, folk customs, and ritual etiquettes. Feng Jicai's *The Miraculous Pigtail* depicts urban legends of Tianjin's old quarter. Additionally, his novellas The *Three-Inch Golden Lotus*, *Yin-Yang and the Eight Trigrams*, and *Firing Double Firecrackers*, along with the short story series *City Folk*, foreground cultural vestiges—those "marginal figures and bizarre incidents" rendered in authentic Tianjin dialect and colloquialisms, constituting "genuine Tianjin-flavored fiction"① that has garnered widespread critical attention. This includes Cheng Naishan's *The Book of Daughters* and Yu Tianbai's *The Sinking of Greater Shanghai*, which capture these cities' unique urban landscapes. The characters epitomize quintessential metropolitan lifestyles. In these works, the city transcends its traditional role as mere literary backdrop—it becomes an indispensable spatial construct that actively shapes the protagonists' identities.

By the mid-1980s, a new wave of urban-conscious literature emerged in contemporary Chinese letters. Works like Liu Sola's *You Have No Choice*, Xu Xing's *Variations Without a Theme*, and Wang Shuo's *The Troubleshooters* epitomized this movement—their narratives pulsating with metropolitan alienation and avant-garde experimentation. These works introduced urban youth imbued with modernist consciousness. *You Have No Choice* portrays conservatory prodigies squandering their talent—indifferent to practice rooms, numb to ambition. *Variations Without a Theme* delivers deadpan sat-

① Hong Zicheng: *A History of Contemporary Chinese Literature*, Peking University Press, 1999, p. 328.

ire of bourgeois aspirations, while *The Troubleshooters* subverts tradition entirely: its protagonists found 3T Company, spurn paternalistic advice, and perform self-worth through existential play. These characters strive to liberate themselves from grand narratives, reclaiming the mundane yet richly textured existence of ordinary urban dwellers. This trajectory evolves in New Realist Fiction: whether in Chi Li's "Wuhan Citizens" series, Zhang Xin's portrayals of metropolitan consumption spaces (cafés, elite clubs, boutiques, luxury hotels, shopping malls, leisure centers), or Qiu Huadong's Beijing narratives—all interrogate urban lifestyles and cultural ethos through distinct lenses, particularly the material spectacles of white-collar and middle-class romanticized consumerism.

Since the 1990s, an increasing number of writers have consciously turned to urban-themed fiction. Jia Pingwa's 1993 novel *Abandoned Capital*, published by Beijing Publishing House, originated from his longstanding desire to "depict the lives of ordinary citizens within Xi'an's ancient chessboard-grid streets and alleys." Some authors recognized that persisting with rural themes risked alienating younger and foreign readers—effective literary transmission, they argued, required shared urban consciousness as a foundational framework. Thus, this work embodies the author' s aspiration for global literary engagement. Through meticulous research, Jia Pingwa documented Xi' an' s arterial lanes and alleyways, cultural relics, and vernacular daily life, effectively crafting a topographical novel that serves as a fictional local chronicle of 1990s Xi'an. Wang Anyi's 1996 novel *The Song of Everlasting Sorrow* dedicates its opening chapters to minutely woven depictions of Shanghai's longtang alleyways, fluttering pigeons, and neighborhood gossip—textual tapestries** that anchor Wang Qiyao's personal saga to the city's century-spanning history. Recognized as a definitive continuation of Shanghai-style literature, the work bridges intimate biography with urban chronicle. Subsequently, works like Wei Hui's *Shanghai Baby*, Chen Danyan's *A Slow Boat to China*, Cheng Naishan's *Shanghai Tango*, and Jin Yucheng's *Blossoms* have become definitive literary portraits of Shanghai—prompting critic Zhang Qinghua to observe: "In some ways, Shanghai perhaps embodies the most authentic modern urban experience. Its innate cosmopolitanism, libertine hues, and 'feminine' essence preserve an aesthetic texture of softness, mellowness, aqueous fluidity, and sensual permeability."①

Simultaneously, literary scholarship kept pace. Chen Zhao's 1985 essay "Writing Urban Literature with a 'Shanghai Flavor'", published in Shanghai Literature (no. 8, 1985), stands as the earliest contemporary articulation advocating for a distinct Shanghainese style in urban fiction. In this groundbreaking work, Chen emphasized the literary reconstruction of Shanghai's regional character, arguing that urban literature must be examined through its geocultural attributes—thereby pioneering a new critical paradigm. From a contemporary vantage point, Shanghai's literature remains the most intensely

① Zhang Qinghua: "*Urban Writing: Unfolding Within Dilemmas*," Mountain Flowers, no. 3, 2011.

urbanized in China. This stems equally from the city's innate metropolitan character and literary heritage, and from the cumulative labor of generations of writers who have meticulously crafted its textual identity. Take *Blossoms* by Jin Yucheng—winner of the 9th Mao Dun Literature Prize—as an exemplar. Originally serialized on Longtang Net, this novel unfolds a panoramic Shanghai narrative spanning the late 1950s to early 1990s, chronicling social metamorphosis through characters ranging from capitalists to merchants, underground Communists to factory workers, sent-down youth to lawyers. *Blossoms* consciously extends and revitalizes the Shanghai literary tradition from *The Sing-Song Girls of Shanghai* to Eileen Chang (Zhang Ailing), while its Shànghǎi dialect narration intensifies the text's authentic local flavor①.

In 1995, a pivotal discussion titled Urbanization and Literature in Transition—led by Zou Ping, Yang Yang, Yang Wenhu, and others—began interrogating modernity's reliability in defining urban literature, particularly its geocultural dimensions. Yang Yang notably urged attention to literature's spatial distribution: "I've observed that much so-called 'urban literature' in contemporary China scarcely differs from traditional rural writing. Do not assume that the mere presence of skyscrapers, modern transit, or monetary motifs in a work inherently constitutes urban literature. ... When discussing urban literature, we must prioritize the geocultural distribution of literary and

① Zeng Jun: "*The Production of Locality: Shanghai Narrative in 'Blossoms'*," Journal of Central China Normal University (Humanities and Social Sciences), no. 6, 2014.

cultural production, resisting the seduction of material urban facades."[①]

Since the new millennium, scholars have increasingly emphasized the geocultural dimensions of urban literature. Liang Fenglian elevates the discourse on urban regionality to a "root consciousness", arguing that locality constitutes the essence of urban literature, while surface-level urban phenomena remain merely incidental. She posits that essence transcends appearance—only by grasping literature' s core (i.e., geocultural attributes) can "literature extend the soul of a place infinitely through urban time and space.[②]" Shi Zhanjun, in *On the Formation of Chinese-Style Urban Literature*, emphasizes that a distinctly Chinese urban literature marked by geocultural attributes is now emerging. He Shaojun further argues: "As globalization intensifies, the significance of locality becomes paradoxically more pronounced... Writers within specific administrative-geographic spheres develop a sense of belonging to their regions, whose institutional characteristics and dynamic trajectories in turn shape literary praxis."[③] For fiction writing, regionality is not merely the soil from which it grows—it profoundly shapes a novel's cultural character, narrative modes, and character construction.

---

① Zou Ping, Yang Yang, Yang Wenhu, et al.: "*Urbanization and Literature in Transition*," Shanghai Literature, no. 5, 1995.

② Liang Fenglian: "On Bloodline: Discussing the Geocultural Attributes of Urban Literature," in Contemporary Urban Literature in the Context of Globalization, Social Sciences Academic Press, 2007, p. 107.

③ He Shaojun: "The Communal Character of 'New Century Literature': A Case Study of Hubei Literature," Literary Contention, no. 2, 2007.

Beyond this, numerous cities have now brandished the banner of cultivating locally rooted urban literature, leveraging it to curate cultural identities—a phenomenon that has actively stimulated the explicit textual manifestation of urban regionality in literary works. For instance, in early 1994, *Special Zone Literature* in Shenzhen championed the banner of "New Urban Literature", followed by *Guangzhou Literature* promoting "New Lingnan Literature" with a dedicated column for "New Generation Writers". The 1996 Issue 6 of *Special Zone Literature* published proceedings from its "'96 New Urban Literature" Symposium held in Shanghai, marking early scholarly engagement with this literary movement. Participants identified conceptual affinities between "New Citizen Fiction" and "New Urban Literature": First, both acknowledge that literature must mirror societal transformations under market economy reforms, capturing emergent lifestyles and character archetypes. Second, they share a commitment to advancing new aesthetic paradigms rooted in urban modernity. Scholars observed that whether termed "New Urban Literature" or "New Citizen Fiction", these movements primarily represented aspirational frameworks rather than consolidated genres. Notably, *Special Zone Literature* has recently published groundbreaking works that subvert traditional paradigms, achieving remarkable formative-stage success and demonstrating encouraging potential.

At the 2007 Shanghai "Urban Literature Forum", Lu Tianming proposed the concept of "literature's secondary return"—arguing that after discovering their "individual self" (xiao wo), writers must progress toward a "collective self", merging their personal voices into the epochal, populist, and national consciousness. Chen Sihe raised the issue of "new character archetypes" in literature, noting: "In Shanghai, I' ve visited government offices where many officials are new Shanghainese—their stories could redefine urban narratives beyond traditional localism. After graduating from university, they chose to remain in Shanghai. These new Shanghainese—entrepreneurs, street vendors, and property buyers alike—have formed emergent social strata that are reshaping the city. Their distinct cultural profiles markedly differ from native Shanghainese. Thus, constructing new literary archetypes becomes crucial, promising expansive horizons for realist fiction."①

Examining urban literary production through the lens of regionality reveals divergent imaginative geographies across Chinese cities. The nation's urban diversity has furnished writers with abundant creative material—from Beijing's bureaucratic labyrinth and Shanghai' s cosmopolitan hybridity to Wuhan' s riverine vitality, Xi'an's archaeological consciousness, Harbin's Russo-Chinese palimpsests, and Guangzhou's mercantile vernacular. These regionally coded narratives demonstrate how cultural specificity permeates and evolves within literary ecosystems. It can be said that "only by infusing urban studies with human subjectivity and imagination does the city acquire emotional resonance—becoming simultaneously ancient and rejuvenated. Conversely, when we strive to articulate a city's past and present through text,

① Lu Tianming: "Literature's Secondary Return and the Spirit of the 'Shi'," Jiefang Daily, March 18, 2007.

imagery, and cultural memory, its essence achieves perpetual regeneration."① For younger generations of writers, the city has become an inseparable part of their lived experience. As Beijing-raised post-80s (balinghou) writer Huo Yan observes: "Writers of the 1950s, even while living in cities, remained nostalgically tied to rural life. I, by contrast, consciously engage with urban themes—what they sought to escape is precisely my existential foundation. I cannot imagine life beyond the city; though it may be cold and impersonal, it has not yet become monstrous."②

In summary, while urban literature has flourished, significant challenges persist. "Compared to the literarily revitalized cities like Xi' an, Harbin, and Wuhan, most Chinese cities remain ambiguously defined in their geocultural distinctiveness. The uneven scholarly and creative attention given to urban imaginaries starkly contradicts China' s vast urban diversity and complex regional attributes."③ For contemporary literary scholars, research on urban literature remains disproportionately focused on the "Beijing School" and "Shanghai School", leaving much of urban literary production in a state of critical obscurity. Many regional urban narratives remain underexplored, and scholarly discourse often fails to engage meaningfully with evolving creative

---

① Chen Pingyuan: "*Beijing Memories and Remembering Beijing*," Social Sciences of Beijing, no. 1, 2005.

② Huo Yan: "*How I Came to Know Myself*," October, no. 4, 2013.

③ Chen Pingyuan, David Der-wei Wang, and Shang Wei (eds.): *Late Ming and Late Qing: Historical Inheritance and Cultural Innovation*, Hubei Education Press, 2002, p. 383.

practices—revealing significant methodological gaps in the field. Consequently, Henan's literary landscape lacks both Beijing's rich cultural sedimentation and Shanghai's robust modern industrial-commercial framework. Its geographically median and conservative positioning further compounds the issue, resulting in sparse urban literary depictions and lagging scholarly engagement—factors that collectively sustain Henan's urban literature in a state of persistent ambiguity.

3. The Current State of Henan Urban Literature

Historically and geographically, Henan corresponds to the ancient Yuzhou, the central province of China' s Nine Divisions, hence its abbreviation "Yu". Known as the "Central Province" and the "Central Plains", it is one of the cradles of Chinese civilization, earning the adage "The history of Henan constitutes half of Huaxia history." Henan stands as a monumental pillar in China' s historical landscape, boasting four of the nation' s Eight Great Ancient Capitals: Luoyang, a 13-dynasty capital; Kaifeng, an 11-dynasty hub; Anyang, which served seven dynasties; and Zhengzhou, the Xia-Shang dynastic seat — alongside culturally rich cities like Shangqiu, Nanyang, Xuchang, and Puyang. This concentration makes Henan the province with the most dynastic capitals, the longest cumulative tenure as a political center, and the highest density of ancient urban heritage in Chinese history. Its layered past encompasses the dawn of Xia-Shang-Zhou civilization, the intellectual flourish of the Wei-Jin period, the territorial might of Han-Tang empires, and the bustling urbanism of the Song era. Such stratified historical sedimentation and cultural multiplicity forge Henan's unparalleled role in China's civilizational narrative. Ban Gu's *Rhapsody on the Eastern Capital* vividly depicts Luoyang during the Eastern Han dynasty. Similarly, Yang Kan's *Rhapsody on the Imperial Domain*, Song Qi's *Rhapsody on the Royal Territory*, Zhou Bangyan's *Rhapsody on the Magnificent Capital*, and Li Changmin's *Grand Rhapsody on the Vast Capital* collectively glorified the Song dynasty capitals. Liu Zihui's poetic cycle Memories of Bianjing nostalgically evokes the splendor of Dongjing, while *Along the River During the Qingming Festival* masterfully captures its urban bustle. During this golden age, Luoyang and Xuchang emerged as thriving cultural hubs, celebrated in the saying: "Between Xu and Luò dwell extraordinary talents."

Following the Northern Song dynasty, prolonged warfare and the Yuan dynasty's diversion of the Grand Canal to Shandong precipitated Kaifeng's precipitous decline—stripping it of its triple status as political hub, cultural nexus, and logistical lifeline, thereby triggering Henan's comprehensive socioeconomic collapse. Han Guohe's Zhengda Historical Studies Library: Examination of "Central Plains" History and Culture analyzes the multidimensional causes of Henan's decline. During the Wei-Jin and Northern-Southern Dynasties periods, the Central Plains endured prolonged warfare. Subsequent conflicts—including Song-Jin confrontations, Mongol ascendancy, and late

Yuan/Ming peasant revolts—all centered on this region as a primary battleground. The relocation of political capitals further accelerated its socioeconomic marginalization. In the modern era, the south-to-north and west-to-east permeation of Western civilization further exacerbated the decline of Henan, long the core of the Central Plains. Additionally, "wars and natural disasters impoverished the region's populace, fostering either reckless bravery among the strong or fatalistic conservatism among the weak. Unlike the south, the Central Plains—especially post-Ming dynasty—remained dominated by smallholder farming economies anchored in self-sufficient peasants. ... Neo-Confucianism entrenched deeply here, its inherently conservative ethos (contrasted with xinxue idealism) demanding rigid social conformity."①

Subsequently, despite a modest revival in modern literature—exemplified by renowned writers like Shi Tuo gathering in Kaifeng during the Republican era—rural themes persistently dominated the literary landscape. This trend reflected Henan's agrarian identity and peripheral geography, distant from treaty ports and metropolises. Shi Tuo's *The Chronicle of Orchard Town* nevertheless carved a literary legacy within the Beijing School tradition, bridging regional roots with modernist aesthetics. Thereafter, aligned with shifts in national ideology, rural literature remained the dominant literary current—a persistence that endured until the post-New Era period, when

① Han Guohe et al.: *Examination of "Central Plains" History and Culture*, Elephant Press, 2012, p. 188.

literature began its aesthetic reorientation. With rapid urbanization, waves of writers migrated to cities, joining established urban authors to form a new vanguard of urban literary production, collectively redefining China's textual landscape. This epochal and creative transition resonates with the 19th-century prophecy of a renowned American novelist-critic: "The intensifying dichotomy between urban and rural life will soon manifest in regional fiction—a genre that, rooted in local color, will dramatize its tragedies and comedies against the panoramic backdrop of our nation, while those flawed yet literarily vibrant cities mushroom across the land."① Since the New Era, urban literature has emerged as a literary manifestation of China's urbanization, with cities themselves generating new spatial imaginaries for life's possibilities. At its core, urban literature expands the imaginative horizons of social existence, offering multifaceted visions of contemporary reality.

Henan writer Zhang Yigong, a seasoned journalist and editor, demonstrated acute news sensitivity and an exceptional grasp of zeitgeist awareness. His short story Black Boy's Photo Session (Heiwa Zhaoxiang) won the 1982 National Outstanding Short Story Award, exemplifying how reportorial precision merged with literary innovation during China's reform era. The work centers on a temple fair—a newly agglomerated urban space—where modern elements converge. Heiwa, a rural youth celebrated as a model of prosperous peasantry, encounters various novelties at the fair, even playacting a phone

---

① (U.S.) Hamlin Garland: *Crumbling Idols*, trans. Liu Baoduan et al., in American Writers on Literature, SDX Joint Publishing Company, 1984, p. 92.

call with an American, and ultimately has his photograph taken, forging a symbolic connection between selfhood and modernity. Later, Zhang Yigong's novel *The Fading Posthouse* (published by Changjiang Literature & Art Press, 2002) revitalizes Kaifeng's urban memory through narrative recollection, weaving together elements such as Guziqu (a traditional drum-accompanied folk art) and familial sagas, emerging as a distinctive literary portrayal of city life.

Yan Lianke's novel series Chronicles of Dongjing's Marginal Figures (Dongjing being the Northern Song Dynasty name for present-day Kai-feng)—including Living Wild (also titled Lu Yao or Cockfighting), The Cel-ebrated Courtesan Li Shishi and Her Descendants, and others—depicts the cultural milieu of Kaifeng. Cockfighting depicts Kaifeng's folk tradition of competitive rooster battles. From emperors and generals to commoners, en-thusiasts of the sport "live with cunning detachment," finding in the training and waging of these fights "a remarkably seamless way to pass the time." Living Wild portrays the life of the renowned "gang leader" Lu Yao during the late Qing and early Republican era. Rising from beggary, Lu embodied chivalrous righteousness, mobilizing fellow beggars to outwit the wealthy and living a life of unbridled defiance. His funeral procession drew massive crowds, a testament to his legacy. This novel series showcases the author' s mastery in depicting the lives of societal outcasts and urban subcultures, earning acclaim as "a landmark achievement in contemporary street-smart cultural fiction"①. It has also become a literary vessel preserving Kaifeng' s historical memory. "A single city wears many faces: one carved by swords—the city of politics; another built of stone—the city of architecture; yet another amassed with gold—the city of economy; and finally, one sketched in words—the city of literature."②

Chen Tiejun's *Old Miscellany* chronicles tales of Zhengzhou during the Republican era. Adopting the perspective of a storyteller active in the pre-Liberation Laofengang district, the work recounts a series of extraordinary adventures among common folk navigating the margins of society. Through these picaresque narratives, it unveils long-buried historical fragments of Zhengzhou as a city. The work teems with characters from all walks of life—newcomers like Westerners and missionaries, chivalrous figures from folk traditions, and ordinary citizens—while also documenting the origins of Zhengzhou's time-honored businesses. It stands as a strikingly unconventional urban narrative. In contrast to such historical retrospection, an increasing number of works now directly engage with the emerging modern city. Li Peifu's *City White Paper* and *City Lights* confront the psychological fragmentation experienced during post-reform reurbanization, exposing the

---

① Wang Qingsheng (ed.), *A History of Contemporary Chinese Literature*, Central China Normal University Press, 1999, p.372.

② Chen Pingyuan, "*Imagining Beijing's Past and Present: An Interview with Xinhua Journalist Liu Jiang*," Journal of Beijing Normal University (Social Science Edition), no. 4, 2005.

struggles born of urban-rural entanglements. His subsequent works, such as *Waiting for the Soul*—inspired by the rise and fall of Zhengzhou's Asia Department Store—persistently explore this thematic terrain, depicting the tragic consequences of unrestrained human souls in urban development. *The Book of Life*, winner of the Mao Dun Literature Prize, opens with the metaphor of a seed taking root in urban soil, encapsulating the vicissitudes of city existence. Works like Tian Zhonghe's novella *Tomorrow's Sun*, Zhang Yu's novel *Weakness*, and Xing Junji's reportage *Zhengzhou Commerce Wars* collectively present multifaceted portrayals of urban life.

Shao Li has also produced numerous works imbued with urban consciousness, such as *My Quality of Life* and *Minghui's Christmas*. Published in 2002 by People's Literature Publishing House, *My Quality of Life* was shortlisted for the Mao Dun Literature Prize. The narrative begins by introducing the grandmother's urban, aristocratic background—displaced to the countryside by war, she pins all her hopes on Wang Qilong. Later, he leaves rural life through university admission and, through a twist of fate, becomes a government official, believing he can fulfill his grandmother's aspirations. Yet, she still urges him to venture further beyond, while Wang Qilong bears a physical marker of his rural origins: the same toe bone structure as his fellow villagers. This trait becomes a recurring symbol, starkly contrasted with the cosmopolitan sophistication of urban-bred women in the latter part of the story, reinforcing a binary opposition between city and countryside. *My Quality of Life* employs a confessional narrative style to probe the spiritual construction of urban dwellers, framing their psychological struggles through intimate first-person encounters.

By contrast, the novella *Minghui's Christmas*—a meditation on metropolitan existence—adopts a more subdued and lingering tone, inviting contemplative reading. Minghui, a rural girl, was the daughter of the village's women's association director. Consistently top-ranked academically—the village's standout student—she suffered the humiliation of failing the national college entrance exam (gaokao). Witnessing the glittering urban transformations of former village girls, she too resolved to migrate to the city. There, she entered the most immediately lucrative sector available—massage services—ultimately funding her urban dream through sex work. The narrative reaches its climax when Minghui, having moved in with Li Yangqun on Christmas Day and seemingly become the mistress of his urban world, believes a new life has begun. Yet at the following year's Christmas celebration, as Li reunites with his childhood friends—confident, glamorous city girls—Minghui observes his effortless assimilation into their world. It is in this moment she realizes her own irrevocable exclusion from the city's fabric, leading to her quiet, despairing suicide. Yet, paradoxically, Li Yangqun remains perplexed: Why did she have to die? The work's unflinching interrogation of marginalized lives—particularly their psychological fragility—pierces the reader' s conscience. Here lies the tragedy of a woman whose innate dignity was systematically crushed by the city.

Qiao Ye's debut novel, *I Truly Love You,* depicts twin sisters corrupted by urban materialism. Critic Lei Da praised the novel for exposing "the brutal experiences of women sucked into the 'black hole' of urbanization" while maintaining "compassion and poetic idealism." Her non-fiction *Demolition Chronicles* confronts the absurdities of urban renewal, where residents feverishly construct and demolish buildings to maximize compensation. Later works like *The Confession* and *The Pearl Journal* further explore human flaws, with the latter richly embedding Henan's culinary culture.

Li Qingyuan's stories—*Su Rang's Redemption*, *Twenty Years*, *The Lost Kanuo*, and *Night Return*—center on rural-to-urban migrants. As the author admits, these narratives draw from his own journey: "I grew up rural, returned after medical school to open a clinic, then relocated to Zhengzhou for my child's education and shifted from healthcare to cultural entrepreneurship. Naturally, my writing gravitates toward these experiences." Other notable urban portraits include Zhang Yu's *Weakness*, Yang Dongming's *Emotional Animals* series, Mo Bai's *Desire*, Xi Tongfa's *Sparrow Dialogues*, Chen Hongwei's *The Secret of the Triangle*, Sun Yu's female-centric narratives, and Wang Xiaopeng's *The Chess Move*. Together, they offer diverse perspectives on urban youth and contemporary social issues, heralding a creative renaissance driven by writers who increasingly treat cities not just as settings but as lived realities. As China's urbanization accelerates, literature mirrors this transformation—capturing its promises, fractures, and the evolving textures of metropolitan life.

Nan Feiyan's Scorpio and his "My Seven Bureaus and Eight Departments" series have garnered significant attention. His writing has always resisted easy categorization—eschewing nostalgic youth narratives or forced historical reconstructions to directly confront the realities of his generation. As early as 2009, upon the publication of *Red Wine* (published in October) and *Ambiguity* (in Beijing Literature), some were astonished that a *post-80s* writer could produce such a seasoned officialdom novel, marveling at his deft prose and ability to transcend personal experience to capture the subtleties of others' lives. Yet as time passed and more substantial works like *Scorpio* and *Leather Anniversary* emerged, the limitations of his earlier writing became apparent—for instance, the diluted portrayal of female characters in *Ambiguity*. Despite Xu Peirong's formidable political background and agency, she transforms into a "helpless little bird" when confronted with love, disregarding her own career to lose herself in Nie Yuchuan's emotional games. Her relentless sacrifices—advising, childcare, cooking, filial duties—embody an excessive virtuous wife and mother archetype, faintly echoing the ghost of Liu Huifang. In *Red Wine*, Jian Fangping boasts an esteemed position (Director of the Departmental Office) and a refined lifestyle—evidenced by his expertise in wine culture—navigating professional matters with effortless finesse. Dubbed "the epitome of old cunning" by the Deputy Director' s son-in-law, he embodies the flawless image of a successful man, self-consciously playing the field across various romantic and matchmaking scenarios. In the story's denouement, just as his romance with the young woman seems poised to culminate in success, an unexpected obstacle arises—a devoutly Christian, almost ascetic, would-be mother-in-law who demands he sacrifice his political career for marriage, abruptly strangling the relationship. Such heavily dramatized plot twists, coupled with the moralizing rhetoric of the prospective mother-in-law, risk lending the narrative a strained sense of artifice.

Scorpio marked a breakthrough. The protagonist Zhu Fangping, weathered by career struggles, encounters the formidable Ding Jingrong—a Scorpio woman who reduces him to "a stray dog" yet ultimately fulfills his ambitions. The tightly woven plot demonstrates expanded narrative scope. By the time of Leather Anniversary, the narrative sheds all dramatic twists, overturning of fortunes, and convoluted plots, unfolding instead into the quiet cadence of everyday life—the fragile existence of ordinary people. This evokes *The Trouble-Shooter*'s Xiao Lin and Xiao Li, whose shattered ideals hasten their plunge into reality, pulling readers into the fragmented, new realist portrayal of life. In its subsequent realist narration, the story grows increasingly melodramatic, its characters reduced to archetypes. Readers may feel these are merely other people's lives—whether the glittering excess of *Tiny Times* or the abject misery of proletarian tales—always separated from ordinary existence by a hazy, glass-like barrier. Yet *Leather Anniversary*'s seemingly subdued narrative manages to resonate deeply. Eschewing jarring pathos or materialistic clashes, it simply traces the mundane lives of unexceptional men and women—neither young nor old, neither high nor low in status. This very quality lends an atypical power to its post-youth writing within the same generational cohort, grounding it in the gritty textures of everyday life.

Yet challenges persist. Homogenization plagues urban literature—overemphasizing modernity while neglecting historical layers. Huang Junye summarizes this as a pervasive phenomenon of repetition: "Writers replicate themselves or each other. When readers open books by different authors, their first impression is déjà vu—from settings, themes, and plots to characters, most works feel nearly identical."[①] This mirrors China's post-1990s urban uniformity: bulldozed neighborhoods birthed identical skylines, eroding local flavor. This has also diminished the diversity and richness of cities, a trend equally reflected in literary works. Writers can only grasp at historical remnants through imagination, constructing narratives like Jia Pingwa's Xi'an in *Ruined City* or Wang Anyi's Shanghai in *The Song of Everlasting Sorrow*. The latter, in particular, is criticized for achieving its continuity with Haipai (Shanghai-style) culture by evacuating historical and political substance. Some scholars attribute this to the exhaustion of urban imagination:

---

① Huang Junye, "The Dilemmas and Pathways of Contemporary Urban Literature Development," Contemporary Literary Review, no. 1, 2004.

"Compared to China's living, breathing cities, the literary imagination of urban space has collapsed into an 'invisible city' shrouded by ideological constructs."①

Simultaneously, the sweeping forces of globalization have eroded urban distinctiveness. As reported by Jiefang Daily (March 23, 2010): "From the pedestrian bridge at No. 283 Huaihai Road's Hong Kong Plaza, one's field of vision is dominated by logos of luxury brands—Louis Vuitton (LV), Tiffany, Zegna, Coach... These global flagship stores are set to cluster in eastern Huaihai Road before the World Expo." ...After all, this is Huaihai Road. Despite the rise of numerous new commercial districts in Shanghai, it remains universally acknowledged as the city's most beautiful, modern, and qiangdiao-laden thoroughfare—a street brimming with distinctive flair and ambiance."② Yet the urban landscapes and modernized centers of nearly every Chinese city now appear inextricably tied to these global brands. Such homogenization has eroded local character, leaving little room for authentic regional flavor to emerge—a phenomenon equally reflected in the urban literary works of Henan Province.

---

① He Ping, "*What is 'My City' and How to 'Literature' It?*," Exploration and Free Views, no. 4, 2011.

② You Chunjie, "*Haute Huaihai Road Set to 'Ignite'*," Jiefang Daily, March 23, 2010.

Academic discourse lags further. Critics still prioritize rural interpretations, overlooking emerging urban voices. Ironically, visual culture adapts faster: Henan's 2018 global promotional video seamlessly connected ancient relics with modern transit networks. Literature awaits scholars willing to excavate these layered urban identities beyond the "Central Plains rural" stereotype.

Chapter 2
The Dominance of Rural Narratives – Urban Literature as a Suppressed Form

Since the First National Congress of Literary and Art Workers established the directive for contemporary literature to serve workers, peasants and soldiers, rural narratives became the mainstream of Chinese literature. From Zhao Shuli's works that established the new direction of Chinese literature, we can observe how "revolutionary literature struggled to make itself appealing to the masses. While traditional China became the target of socialist revolution in spiritual and cultural terms, it paradoxically became the aesthetic ideal that revolutionary literature desperately pursued. This meant that cities representing modern civilization were destined to be aesthetically marginalized - the 'city' strangely became a forgotten corner in cultural and aesthetic expression, a ghost that needed to be exorcised."① From Zhao Shuli's *The Marriage of Xiao Erhei* that combined ordinary people's lives with new marriage policies, to epic works depicting socialist movements like *The Sun Shines Over the Sanggan River*, *The Hurricane and Never Take That Road*, and then to works undertaking class struggle missions like *Never Forget* and *Sentinels Under Neon Lights*, we can see how cities increasingly became demonized as the "other" and targets of class struggle. For Henan province, which suffered through disasters, wars and political movements throughout the 20th century, its cultural ecosystem became even more impoverished, and

① Chen Xiaoming, "Urban Literature: The 'Other' That Cannot Appear," Literature & Art Studies, no. 1, 2006.

urban literature was suppressed beneath the dominant tones of rural narratives.

1. Direction and Transformation

Mao Zedong's "*Talks at the Yan'an Forum on Literature and Art*" and his speech at the First National Congress established the Yan'an artistic direction as the guiding principle for New China's literature and art - serving the masses, workers, peasants and soldiers, while establishing the paradigm of rural writing. According to literary historian Fujii Shōzō, this cultural ecosystem was inherently rural and anti-urban from its very emergence. Yan'an, which at the time absorbed many progressive women from Shanghai and Beijing as well as intellectuals from Nationalist-controlled areas like Chongqing, Guilin and Kunming, was merely a "super village." "The thousands of urban youth who went to Yan'an had no media to express the intellectual class's mission and demands, fundamentally because the foundation that had sustained intellectuals since the late Qing - the city - did not exist here. In this 'super village,' the intellectual class was useless; to secure food and clothing, they had no choice but to leave Yan'an for the liberated areas and engage in Communist propaganda work." This "super village" model gradually spread to other Communist-controlled regions across the country, including Beijing and Shanghai, leading to the decline of literature. Subsequently, works like Ding Ling's *The Sun Shines Over the Sanggan River* and Zhou Libo's *The Hurricane* were created to align with the land reform movement.

The First National Congress represented a collective disillusionment for writers from Nationalist-controlled areas. During this period, Ding Ling was highlighted as a model for "how to integrate with workers, peasants and soldiers." The Congress first arranged for Ding Ling to deliver a keynote speech titled "*From the Masses, To the Masses*". She confidently addressed the issue of "integration with workers, peasants and soldiers" that had been a source of frustration and anxiety for writers from Nationalist-controlled areas:"What problems exist in our initial integration with the masses? I can think of several: First, being guests versus becoming co-owners with the masses... Second, being teachers versus being students... Third, writing for its own sake versus doing the work well... When these problems are properly resolved, one's lifestyle, preferences and emotions naturally transform. The relationship with the masses naturally evolves from distance to unity, from superficial politeness to intimate friendship. You realize the masses you claimed to love before were abstract, and your professed love was false, or at least insincere, because you didn't truly know or understand them. Only then do you genuinely love them - their every breath moves you, you constantly think of them, feel compelled to give them more, and recognize them as your spiritual supporters and encouragers. These people are not individuals - not just this aunt or that uncle - but a collective whole."① This ideological transformation of writers into students was exemplified by Ding Ling, an influential writer

① Ding Ling, "*From the Masses, To the Masses*," in Commemorative Anthology of the All-China Congress of Literary and Art Workers, Xinhua Bookstore, 1950, pp.175-176.

in both Nationalist and Communist areas who completed her ideological remolding in Yan'an. Through this model figure, the overall transformation of new literature and writers was accomplished.

Moreover, "the Yan'an writers—including Chen Xuezhao, Cao Ming, Kang Zhuo, and Kong Jue—were also mobilized at the First Congress as psychological resources for ideological transformation. Their respective speeches ('On the Evolution of Writing Thought,' 'Inspirations from Workers,' 'On the Path of Study,' and 'Going Rural and Creative Practice') collectively articulated this shift in literary consciousness. Such systematic explications of creative metamorphosis were hardly incidental; they demonstrated how the Yan'an intellectual mentality, as a generative resource for the new literary apparatus, had been thoroughly assimilated by the CCP's ideological leadership."①

Simultaneously, certain bourgeois intellectuals were excluded from the Congress. Writers like Shen Congwen, deemed to have "consciously acted as reactionaries," and Xiao Jun, who resisted the spirit of the "Talks" by declaring "Lu Xun is my father, Mao Zedong is merely my elder brother,"② were barred from participation. Even democratic personage Ba Jin, who had

① Si Yanwei, "The First National Congress of Literary and Art Workers and the Formation of the Seventeen-Year Literary Institutional Psyche," Theoretical Studies in Literature and Art, no. 4, 2006.

② Xiao Yunru and Gao Jie, "*Documenting the Yan'an Forum on Literature and Art* (Part 3)," Shaanxi Daily, July 2, 1992.

made no direct contributions to the "revolution," humbly stated at the congress: "I am not here to speak, but to learn." Traditional artist Mei Lanfang admitted: "Hearing the esteemed opinions at this congress makes me realize our theatrical performances require further reform."① Cao Yu's speech was even more modest: "We pay sincere tribute to the liberated areas—their open-mindedness, freedom from personal baggage, integrity and humility. Those who become students of the people then become teachers of the people—we must learn from this transformative experience."② Chen Xuezhao, despite years of work in Yan'an, still felt conscious guilt about her Western literary background, framing her speech as political reformation: "I feel I have been well transformed through learning from workers, peasants and soldiers, continuing to purge Western literary influences, serving as the people's attendant, and becoming Chairman Mao's good student."

The absolute affirmation and elevation of "worker-peasant-soldier literature" practiced in the liberated areas under Mao's "*Talks*" deprived writers from liberated and Nationalist-controlled areas of any equal dialogue platform. As Zhou Yang stated: "Chairman Mao's '*Talks at the Yan'an Forum on Literature and Art*' established the direction for New China's literature and art. Writers from liberated areas consciously and resolutely implemented

① Mei Lanfang, "*The Urgent Need for Further Reform in Our Theater Performances*," in Commemorative Anthology of the All-China Congress of Literary and Art Workers, Xinhua Bookstore, 1950, p.391.

② Xu Ying, "Press Notes from the First National Congress of Literary and Art Workers (Part 2)," Archives & Historiography, no. 2 (2000).

this direction, proving its complete correctness through their collective experience, believing no alternative direction could exist—any other would be erroneous."① The cultural programs arranged during the congress overwhelmingly featured worker-peasant-soldier themes—of 55 theatrical performances, 9 portrayed workers, 19 peasants, 13 soldiers, 1 student, 1 urban citizen, 3 exposed Nationalist-controlled areas' darkness, with only 9 traditional operas.②

Scholar Wang Binbin analyzed the revisions made to the service targets of literature and art between the Yan'an version of the "*Talks*" and the version included in the *Selected Works of Mao Zedong*, revealing different positioning of the petty bourgeoisie.

Our literature and art ought to serve the four categories of people mentioned above. Among these, workers, peasants, and soldiers are primary, while the petty bourgeoisie—though more cultured—are numerically smaller and less revolutionary in resolve. Thus, our cultural work must prioritize the worker-peasant-soldier masses, with the petty bourgeoisie secondary. Never should their order be inverted. Yet herein lies the crux of misunderstanding for some comrades who fail to correctly resolve the fundamental question: For whom are literature and art intended?...

---

① Zhou Yang: "The New People's Literature and Art," in Commemorative Collection of the All-China Congress of Literary and Art Workers, Xinhua Bookstore, 1950, p. 70.

② Theatrical Performances Program, in Commemorative Anthology of the All-China Congress of Literary and Art Workers, Xinhua Bookstore, 1950, p.595.

While in the *Selected Works of Mao Zedong*, it was revised as follows:

Our literature and art must serve the aforementioned four categories of people. To serve these groups effectively, we must adopt the proletarian standpoint—never the petty bourgeois position. Today, writers who cling to individualistic petty bourgeois perspectives cannot authentically serve the revolutionary worker-peasant-soldier masses; their creative focus remains fixated on a narrow stratum of petty bourgeois intellectuals. Herein lies the core dilemma for those comrades still struggling to resolve the fundamental question: For whom should literature and art exist?

This reflects shifting ideological demands on the petty bourgeoisie across different historical periods. While classified as part of "the people," they were excluded from the worker-peasant-soldier alliance, gradually becoming targets of post-1949 exile and re-education. As Li Tuo observes: "What fundamentally distinguishes 'worker-peasant-soldier literature'? Unlike 'popular literature' which merely writes for the masses, 'worker-peasant-soldier literature' requires authors to undergo self-reform—actively transferring their class standpoint to that of the masses. This constitutes its defining feature."①

In tandem with the worker-peasant-soldier literature's valorization of rural culture was its deep suspicion of urban lifestyles. The 1950 short story

① Tang Xiaobing (ed.), *Reinterpretations: Popular Literature and Ideology* (expanded ed.), Peking University Press, 2007, p.258.

Between Us, a Couple—published in *People's Literature* (no. 1) and initially praised (even adapted into film)—was swiftly condemned for its negative portrayal of a peasant-born wife. Meanwhile, works like *Never Forget* and *Sentinels Under the Neon Lights* were explicitly tasked with dramatizing the Two-Line Struggle, reinforcing ideological vigilance against urban corruption. As Cong Shen recalled the creative process behind *Never Forget*: "After the CCP's 10th Plenary Session communiqué① in October 1962, I gained concrete understanding of certain social phenomena—'the force of habit among millions,' 'the petty proprietors' daily, trivial, elusive corrosive activities,' and 'how petty bourgeois spontaneity encircles, infiltrates, and corrupts the proletariat from all sides.' These, I realized, constituted the class struggle during the transitional phase from socialism to communism." The Communiqué of the Tenth Plenary Session of the Eighth Central Committee illuminated the thematic core of my embryonic play: "The overthrown reactionary ruling class will never reconcile itself to defeat—they invariably seek restoration. Simultaneously, bourgeois influences and residual feudal habits persist in society, alongside spontaneous capitalist tendencies among petty producers. Suddenly, clarity dawned: What I sought to dramatize was precisely this latter form of class struggle." "This class struggle is intricate, cir-

① In September 1962, at the Tenth Plenary Session of the Eighth Central Committee, Mao Zedong reasserted the theory of class struggle, explicitly stating that during the socialist historical stage, "there exists class struggle between the proletariat and the bourgeoisie, and there exists the struggle between the two paths of socialism and capitalism."

cuitous, and fluctuating—at times even intensely violent." I attempted to apply this theory to real-life dilemmas, and the more I reflected, the more I recognized its "kaleidoscopic complexity." "I resolved to chronicle a battlefield where proletarian and bourgeois ideologies clash, championing the former while condemning the latter."

The play *Sentinels Under the Neon Lights* was adapted from the story of the "Good Eighth Company on Nanjing Road." The very title, juxtaposing "neon lights" with "sentinels," implicitly reveals the contradiction and opposition between these two symbolic elements. Neon lights served as emblems of urban decadence and moral corruption—a visual trope established in early Chinese cinema. In *The Goddess*, neon signs flickered with cold luminescence against the gloomy metropolitan nightscape, while later urban films like *City Scenes* and *Street Angels* consistently portrayed them as emitting "flame-like red and phosphorescent green flares."① These artificial lights, described by critics as "steel beams supporting the nocturnal system of public eroticism and material consumption, became synonymous with modern commodities like automobiles, Western-style houses, sofas, perfumes, and high heels—all signifiers of problematic modernity."②Both *Never Forget* and *Sentinels Under the Neon Lights* received high praise from top leadership and

① Mao Dun, *Midnight*, People's Literature Publishing House, 1960, p.1.

② Nie Wei, "'Sentinels Under the Neon Lights': Urban Sensibility Shrouded in War Ideology," Contemporary Cinema, no. 6 (2005).

were swiftly promoted nationwide. Their success reinforced the revived discourse of class struggle and reestablished urban symbols as negative representations, ultimately marginalizing cities from mainstream literary narratives during this period.

2. Contemporary Cultural Ecology of Henan

Since the 20th century, Henan has consistently been characterized as an agricultural region, disaster-prone zone, and war-torn area. According to Professor Lu Shuyuan's analysis: "The Central Plains historically served as the contested territory for military campaigns from all directions—the so-called 'strategic land coveted by all.' With few natural defenses, the region witnessed endless back-and-forth battles between opposing forces, forcing its inhabitants to survive in the interstices of conflict. Over time, this bred a self-preservationist cultural mentality: psychological insularity, passive competition, situational compliance, and forced adaptability. Yet this volatile, merciless environment also forged generations of political elites—strategists skilled in maneuvering, negotiation, and statecraft... On this land, a 'power culture' flourished with particular intensity."[①] This turbulent political landscape corresponded with an increasingly desolate cultural sphere. In the 1940s, as China endured foreign invasion and civil strife alongside succes-

---

① Lu Shuyuan, *Ecological Literary Studies*, Shaanxi People's Education Press, 2000, pp.329-330.

sive natural disasters, Kaifeng experienced a brief "cultural renaissance." Diasporic Henan writers like Shi Tuo, Yu Gengyu, and Yao Xueyin returned, while even poet Niu Han and his wife joined Kaifeng's Zhengyi Daily as editors. However, war soon dispersed this intellectual gathering: 17-year-old Wei Wei left Zhengzhou for Shanxi's revolutionary base in 1937; Liu Zhixia departed for Yan'an's Anti-Japanese Military and Political University in 1938; Li Ji exited Tanghe for the Luochuan branch of the same institution. This brain drain exacerbated Henan's cultural deterioration. As scholar Liu Zengjie lamented in Fifty Turbulent Years: Henan Literature in the First Half of the 20th Century: "Most writers became subservient, strictly conforming to ideological uniformity. The rare bold innovators who forged unique artistic paths met grim fates—ranging from reprimands to livelihood-threatening punishments. Ultimately, creative vitality evaporated, and a make-do mentality mass-produced mediocre works devoid of edges."①

The deterioration of cultural ecology corresponded with a series of shocking historical tragedies. Liu Zhenyun's novel Remembering 1942 revisits the horrific Henan famine of that year, which the author called his "only non-fiction work." His hometown, Yanjin County, was among the worst-hit areas by drought and locust plagues. According to historical records, "From the summer of 1942 to the spring of 1943, Henan suffered a catastrophic

① Liu Zengjie, "Fifty Turbulent Years: Henan Literature in the First Half of the 20th Century," in Spiritual Central Plains: 20th-Century Henan Literature, Henan University Press, 2002, p.35.

drought, the horrors of which defied description. Most summer and autumn harvests across the province failed entirely. The drought was followed by locust plagues. Five million victims—20% of Henan's population—were affected. The quadruple calamities of flood, drought, locusts, and Tang Enbo's armies ravaged all 110 counties."[①] "Starving peasants ate tree bark and roots, with corpses littering the fields. Women's market prices plummeted to one-tenth of pre-famine levels, while male laborers' value dropped by a third. Central China became a barren wasteland—over three million Henan residents perished."

To reconstruct this history, the author interviewed survivors including his grandmother, Uncle Huazhua, landlord elements Fan Kejian and Guo Youyun, Commissioner Han, and Granny Cai. Yet their fragmented memories proved unreliable—even the famine's exact year eluded recollection. "Grandma, fifty years ago, the great drought killed so many!" prompted the author. "Many years saw starvation deaths—which one do you mean?" she replied. When pressed for details, Uncle Huazhua snapped: "People starved to death, and you demand specifics!" This forced the author to reconstruct events through archival materials rather than oral history.

This historical tragedy was documented in reports like *A True Record of the Henan Disaster* by *Ta Kung Pao* war correspondent Zhang Gaofeng in February 1943, which chronicled the spreading catastrophe and desperate

① Liu Zhenyun, *Remembering 1942*, Changjiang Literature & Art Press, 2012, p.4.

survival measures—eating tree bark, straw, and firewood. Consequently, thirty million victims fled as refugees. *Time* magazine reporters traveled counter to the refugee exodus, documenting how people escaped by clinging to trains or walking, with many crushed to death during train-jumping attempts. The situation deteriorated to selling children and even cannibalism. Journalist Theodore White photographed dogs feeding on human corpses. Yet these humanitarian catastrophes were silenced and deliberately ignored amid "greater events."

As Liu Zhenyun notes: "To the leadership, 'three million starving deaths in the East wouldn't affect history.'" For Chiang Kai-shek, ordinary lives meant nothing compared to China's Allied status, the war against Japan, and Kuomintang factional struggles. Concurrent global events—Soong Ching-ling's U.S. visit, Gandhi's hunger strike, the Battle of Stalingrad, even Churchill's cold—made history books, while Henan's three million famine deaths were forgotten. This confirms the disaster was as much man-made as natural: despite crop failures since 1940, heavy grain requisitions continued for military supplies; the 1942 drought's total crop failure met with token relief efforts. The entire relief operation became a farce—"a farce borne by victims while provincial officials served lavish banquets for White and Forman."[①]

---

① Wang Xiaohong, "Remembering 1942: We Are All Descendants of the Victims," Prosecutorial View, no. 6, 2012.

The post-1949 "Xinyang Incident" marked another tragic chapter. Henan's economy and living standards collapsed—agricultural regression saw 1960 grain yields drop 1.65 billion jin below 1951 levels. Oil, cotton, pork and light industrial production all declined, with annual per capita pork consumption at merely 0.15kg. Birth rates plunged from 35‰ (1957) to 14‰, while mortality rates soared from 11.8‰ to 39.6‰—a net population decrease of 1.61 million. Central-South Bureau First Secretary Tao Zhu, investigating Xinyang and eastern Henan, angrily condemned local leaders after seeing mass edema from starvation: "Henan's cadres only fear capitalism!" *1960 Statistical Abstract* shows Henan's population dropped by 1.25 million (49.7 to 48.45 million) from 1958-1960, corroborated by *1963 Statistical Abstract data* (4.943 to 4.818 million).[①] Witnessing Guangshan County's universal mourning, Li Xiannian told Wang Renzhong: "I didn't weep at the Western Route Army's defeat, but seeing this broke my heart!"[②]

At the dawn of the New Era, Henan writer Zhang Yigong's short story *The Criminal Li Tongzhong*—based on the Xinyang Incident—was published despite significant political risks. After numerous twists and turns, it

---

① Li Ruojian, "A Study of Population Statistics in Henan Province, 1957-1963," South China Population, no. 6, 2016.

② Xinyang Prefecture Party History Office, "*A Complete Account of the 'Xinyang Incident'*," in *The 'Great Leap Forward' Movement in Henan*, compiled by the Henan Provincial Committee Party History Research Office, CPC History Publishing House, 2006, p.459.

ultimately won the National Outstanding Short Story Award. Set in Lijia Village during the Great Leap Forward, the story depicts 490 villagers facing complete food depletion, having consumed even the elm bark. Li Tongzhong saves the villagers by opening the state grain reserve, violating laws to become a "criminal." Breaking through the narrative constraints of ultra-leftism, the work exposed the people's suffering under leftist ideological currents during the "Seventeen Years" period (1949-1966), establishing itself as a pioneering work of "Reflection Literature." Zhu Zhai's 1984 *Compendium of Chinese New Literature and Art: Theoretical Volume II* cited critic Yan Gang's analysis: "*The Criminal Li Tongzhong* ventures into long-taboo territory fraught with political dangers. Amid skepticism and neglect, our literary critics rose to defend it—confronting every vulnerable contradiction: law versus morality, organizational obedience versus emergency response, state property versus saving lives, hero versus criminal. With rigorous logic, they proved Li Tongzhong a hero rather than a criminal." The critique invoked Marx's praise of Prometheus to sanctify Li Tongzhong as a "noble saint and martyr" in Marxist terms, armor-plating this noble image with ideological legitimacy.① This reflected Zhang Yigong's journalistic conscience and profound reckoning with historical tragedy.

① Yan Gang, "Zhang Yigong and 'The Story of Criminal Li Tongzhong'," Yanhuang Chunqiu, no. 6 (2016).

3. "Never Take That Road"

Li Zhun's *Never Take That Road* was among the earliest works by a Henan writer to achieve nationwide acclaim after the founding of the New China. Born Li Tiesheng on July 4, 1928, in Xiatun Village (now part of Mengjin County, Luoyang City), Henan Province, Li Zhun grew up in a family of rural schoolteachers and minor landowners. At age six, he began attending Matun Primary School half a mile from home, where he adopted "Li Zhun" as his academic name. During elementary school, he studied foundational texts like the *Three Character Classic*, *Standards for Being a Good Student*, and *Family Instructions of the Zhu Family*. After graduating from primary school in 1940, Li enrolled at Changdai Town's Dade Middle School in Luoyang County but had to drop out after his first year due to Henan's catastrophic 1942 drought and his family's resulting poverty. Fleeing as a refugee to Xi'an, he endured months of hardship that exposed society's darkest realities before returning home that autumn. With no school to attend, Li pursued classical literature under his grandfather's tutelage, studying the *Records of the Grand Historian*, *Gems of Chinese Prose*, *Anthology of Yuefu Poetry*, *Combined Interpretations of Tang Poetry*, *Classified Collection of Ancient Prose*, *The Romance of the West Chamber*, and *Suiyuan Poetry Talks*. This rigorous self-education laid a profound foundation in traditional literature. In 1943, financial desperation forced Li to apprentice at Luoyang Station's Hengyuan Salt Depot, where colleague Li Baocai inspired him to borrow books from Luoyang's "Deaf Man's Bookstore." There, he discovered Tolstoy, Turgenev, Balzac, Dickens, Lu Xun, Mao Dun, and Ba Jin—exposure that dramatically expanded his artistic horizons and cemented his literary passion. By 1945, Li became a postal clerk in Matun Town. Delivering mail gave him daily access to newspapers and magazines—he read five or six papers daily and two to three monthly periodicals, broadening his understanding of society. He often wrote letters for illiterate farmers, gaining intimate knowledge of hundreds of peasant households and townspeople—barbers, tofu sellers, night watchmen, butchers, musicians, and fortune-tellers. As he later told friends: "I never attended college—society was my university." These vivid characters from all walks of life would later populate his fiction.①

On November 20, 1953, Li Zhun's debut short story *Never Take That Road* was published in *Henan Daily*, sparking widespread social impact for its sharp critique of rural socialist revolution. On January 26, 1954, *Urban Daily* reprinted the full text with an editorial note: "This story vividly depicts the triumph of socialist ideology over spontaneous capitalist tendencies among peasants—one of the finest rural-themed short stories in recent years." The Central-South Bureau of the CPC Central Committee issued a special notice on March 27, 1954, titled *Directive on Reprinting Li Zhun's Short*

① Xiong Kunjing, "The Context and Legacy of the Short Story 'We Must Not Take That Road'," Dangshi Bocai, no. 12 (2014).

Story, ordering: "All regional and provincial/municipal newspapers must reprint this work using *People's Daily*'s edited version and editorial framework. Rural cadres and intellectuals should study this story, which may be adapted into local performance materials for village theater troupes." Propelled by this official endorsement, *Never Take That Road* was subsequently reprinted by 38 national publications. The story's explosive reception established Li Zhun's reputation overnight—by 1955, he was transferred to the Henan Federation of Literary and Art Circles as a professional writer and elected to Henan's First People's Congress.

In April of the same year, *Never Take That Road* was republished by Henan People's Publishing House, while Popular Reading Press simultaneously released a standalone edition, which went through four printings by 1959. The story was subsequently adapted into various artistic forms, including films, stage plays, Bangzi opera, Zhuizi opera, Min opera, Yu opera, Meihu opera, and comic books. Between April 1954 and July 1955 alone, the story was adapted into multiple comic book versions by Shanghai New Art Publishing House, Mass Art Publishing House, Henan People's Publishing House, and Morning Flowers Art Publishing House. The initial print run by Shanghai New Art Publishing House reached 22,000 copies, generating widespread social impact.The story is regarded as the first literary work after the founding of New China to depict the ideological and political struggle between two paths in socialist rural transformation. Later works such as Zhao Shuli's *Sanliwan* and Liu Qing's *The Builders* were considered influenced by *Never Take That Road.*

The story's sensational impact stemmed from its accurate grasp of political direction and policy. Mao Zedong had long been wary of class polarization in rural areas. In his *Report on Agricultural Cooperativization*, he described the situation as follows: "In recent years, capitalist tendencies in the countryside have grown daily, with new rich peasants emerging everywhere. Many well-off middle peasants strive to become rich peasants, while poor peasants, lacking production resources, remain impoverished—some in debt, others forced to sell or rent out their land. If this trend continues, class polarization in rural areas will only worsen." Li Zhun's precise alignment with this policy stance allowed the story to unequivocally declare that the capitalist path must not be taken. His work thus became a literary manifesto for socialist rural transformation, reinforcing the ideological campaign against "spontaneous capitalist tendencies" in the countryside.

The story begins with Zhang Shuan, weakened by labor struggles, deciding to sell the fertile land allocated to his family during land reform. Lao Ding, an experienced farmer still influenced by old ideologies, aspires to become a "landowner" and plots to buy the plot to establish family wealth for his descendants. However, his elder son Dongshan, a Party member, opposes the purchase, leading to a father-son conflict. Dongshan attempts to persuade his father: "Dad! In the past, landlords wished for the poor to stay poor forever. But now, we help each other. You've suffered—you know how it feels.

We can't take the same path as those landlords." Eventually, with collective support, Zhang Shuan overcomes his hardships. Lao Ding, moved by this solidarity, voluntarily lends Zhang Shuan 300,000 yuan (old currency). The story concludes with Lao Ding "walking step by step toward the rising sun in the east."

As Pan Xulan observed: "Li Zhun possessed the political sensitivity crucial for a revolutionary writer. Having long immersed himself in rural life, he understood peasants deeply and held himself to strict standards. Guided by Mao Zedong Thought and Party policies across different periods, he observed life through the lens of class struggle. This cultivated his ability to detect emerging contradictions before they gained widespread attention—to discern significant shifts in seemingly ordinary events and reflect new problems in reality."①

Following the publication of *Never Take That Road*, China launched a sweeping agricultural collectivization campaign that lasted decades. This historical chapter was repeatedly depicted in works like *The Builders*, *Sanliwan*, *Great Changes in a Mountain Village*, *Sunny Skies*, *My First Superior*, *The Story of Li Shuangshuang*, *New Acquaintances*, *The Unfettered Hands*, *The Pragmatist Pan Yongfu*, *On the Sands*, *The Legend of 'Old Resolute'*, *Sister Lai*, and *The Golden Road*. These works fully captured the social transformations of that era, creating numerous "political supermen" and "socialist

---

① Pan Xulan, "On Li Zhun's Fiction," Literary Review, no. 5, 1964.

new men." However, in the post-New Era period, these narratives became subjects of historical reflection—tragedies that led to social stagnation, low productivity, rural impoverishment, and generations haunted by hunger. Naturally, *Never Take That Road* also faced scrutiny in the New Era. In the early 1980s, Li Zhun responded candidly during a visit to Yunnan: "Evaluating mutual aid and cooperativization is the task of politicians and historians. As a writer, I can only speak with artistic conscience." For him, this conscience meant "reflecting the vibrant pulse of life and voicing the people's aspirations. Regardless of past, present, or future, no matter how society changes, I firmly believe the Chinese people must never return to the path of exploitation, where the rich feed on the poor! Writers and artists, too, must avoid becoming spiritual aristocrats. The road of detachment from life is impassable."①

He added: "Writers must think independently. The Cultural Revolution's bitter lesson boils down to three words: 'Don't worship idols'—that's our greatest takeaway." At over fifty, he reflected: "After so many cycles, so many tears, so much emotional investment, and so many blows, I've finally grasped the meaning of 'no doubts.'" This wisdom came through painful experience: "In the 1950s, we all toed the party line—writing about 'bound-foot women' and 'black societies' as instructed. Looking back, it's shameful to have wasted precious energy on such worthless depictions." With regret, he concluded: "These questions weigh on me. We lost so many good years.

① Zeng Zhennan, "*Meditations in the Museum of Modern Literature*," Guangming Daily, September 28, 2000.

It's not about assigning blame but learning from the past." He remarked: "Writers must think independently. The 'cultural revolution' exacted such a heavy price—the lesson learned boils down to three words: 'no more idols.' That is its greatest legacy." And further: "I'm now in my fifties. Only after countless cycles of repetition, endless tears, squandered emotions, and repeated beatings have I earned the right to say 'no illusions.'" His insights were forged through painful experience. He reflected: *"In the 1950s, we all toed the orthodox line—whatever the authorities dictated, we wrote. Re-reading those pieces about 'bound-foot women' and 'black societies' now fills me with shame. To think I squandered my creative energy on such worthless depictions!"* And soberly added: "These regrets weigh on me deeply—so many prime years lost. Ours is not to settle scores, but to reckon honestly."①

Based on this reflection, Li Zhun raised the issue of "campaign literature," observing: "Following China's thirty-year pattern, literary works emerged in schools—like yellow croaker migrations—with each political campaign: one batch for land reform, another for the Marriage Law, another for resisting America and aiding Korea, yet another for collectivization. Li Zhun did not seek to negate the validity of such principles. He maintained that "so long as your ideological line is correct and revolutionary, your work shall achieve immortality. ... Simply documenting certain truths of our time will inevitably produce works imbued with historical authenticity—and vivid

① Sun Su, "*Li Zhun in Transition*," Journal of Zhengzhou University (Philosophy and Social Sciences Edition), no. 3, 1983.

characters will naturally emerge."①

Li Zhun did not entirely dismiss this pattern's rationale. He maintained: "As long as your ideological line is correct and revolutionary, your work achieves immortality... Recording certain truths preserves the spirit of the times and brings characters to life."

This perspective suggests that post-1949 literature—whether Zhang Yigong's "documentation of life" or Li Zhun's "recording of social realities"—primarily served the needs of specific political campaigns and revolutionary struggles, with limited agency left to writers themselves. In such turbulent times, only radically revolutionary literary forms could thrive. The paucity of creative output during this period is stark: Dr. Zhang Dongxu's research reveals that only 18 full-length novels were published in Henan between 1951 and 1977, illustrating the broader literary stagnation.

4. Li Zhun's Legacy

In the 1950s, Li Zhun's works *Never Take That Road* and *The Story of Li Shuangshuang* sparked nationwide acclaim. Reflecting on his creative origins, Li Zhun explained:

In the autumn of 1953, the Central Committee announced the General Line for the Transition Period, which for the first time proposed that peasants

---

① Ibid.

required socialist education and transformation. This represented a significant leap in understanding compared to the land reform era—peasants were no longer merely "victims" in grievance meetings but were recognized as having a dual nature: they were both hardworking and simple yet also prone to spontaneous capitalist tendencies. At the same time, it was emphasized that the peasant economy stood at a "crossroads"—it could advance toward socialism or revert to capitalism, with the latter being the more familiar path. I was deeply intrigued by the study of peasant class characteristics and read every issue of *Study* magazine for its debates on the topic. Armed with these insights, along with real-life incidents involving my own relatives, I wrote *Never Take That Road.*①

This also highlights Li Zhun's distinctive approach to writing: closely aligning with policy directives. While his works largely fall under ideological literature, we must not overlook the author's sincerity—his genuine belief in the cause and his self-identification as an "authentic social chronicler." However, the unique historical context of that era inevitably impacted the artistic quality of his works, including the widely celebrated *The Story of Li Shuangshuang*. Published in the March 1960 issue of *People's Literature*, this short story introduced the character Li Shuangshuang as a model "socialist new

① Li Zhun, "*Knocking on the Gate of Literature*," in *Knocking on the Gate of Art: Memoirs of Literary and Artistic Masters*, ed. National Committee of the Chinese People's Political Consultative Conference (CPPCC) Cultural and Historical Materials Research Committee. Beijing: China Literature and History Press, 2016, p.99.

person." Born into extreme poverty, Li Shuangshuang endured domestic violence before the founding of New China. She was a woman without a name—referred to by neighbors as "Xiwang's wife" or "Xiwang's woman," by younger villagers as "Sister Xiwang," and by her husband as "the one in my house" or "my little Ju's mother." It wasn't until the Great Leap Forward, when she posted a dazibao (big-character poster), that her name "leaped" onto the communal bulletin boards and provincial newspapers. In this poster, she advocated for the establishment of communal canteens to realize the "leap forward" plan and actively helped set up the village canteen. She also took the initiative to reform her husband's outdated thinking:

"Why do you keep harping on that 'Whitewood Inn of North Mountain'? I don't want to hear it. That was the old society—back then, you were beaten and bullied, and no matter how delicious the food you made was, it was all for those landlords, tyrants, and scoundrels. What did we ever get to eat at home? Our bowls were so empty you could see your reflection in them; we couldn't even knead decent bran buns, and not once during New Year's did we see a single white steamed bun. Now, even if this canteen serves simple meals, it's all for us, the working people. Stop boasting about your past—I believe that if we keep 'leaping forward' like this, someday, when the harvests are abundant, the pigs are fat, and the fish ponds are full, we'll surpass even the fanciest restaurant food you ever made!"

The character of Li Shuangshuang is particularly vibrant and multifaceted. Her bold, decisive, and capable personality traits—markedly different from the submissive image of women in pre-revolutionary China—established her as a radiant figure in contemporary literature. Yet we must not overlook the narrative's core framework: Li Shuangshuang embodies the socialist new woman forged in the Three Red Banners movement. As a standard-bearer of emergent forces, she shoulders the ideological mission of reforming Xi Wang's antiquated mindset. Xi Wang's life philosophy—"If I offend others, they'll offend me"—dictates a cautious creed: "Stay unsullied; harmony is supreme." To Li Shuangshuang, such men "consult the almanac before pissing, and fear a speck of dust might dent their skulls." Xi Wang, perpetually anxious about offending others, naturally feared his wife might do the same—this epitomized the survival philosophy of ordinary peasants. It was precisely this timidity that repeatedly clashed with Li Shuangshuang's fearless pursuit of progress, her character recognizing no authority, whether earthly or divine. As a Henan writer, Li Zhun's prose is vibrant and rich with authentic local flavor, vividly illustrated through subtle details like the evolving ways Li Shuangshuang is addressed by others, as well as Xi Wang's gradual psychological transformation in how he perceives his wife. Moreover, the skillful incorporation of local dialects infuses the work with authentic regional charm. Li Zhun's distinctive writing style, as an integral part of China's literary tradition, has profoundly influenced both the trajectory of post-liberation Chinese literature and the development of Henan's regional literary identity.

During the Cultural Revolution, Li Zhun faced political adversity. In the early years of the New Era, his novel *The Yellow River Flows East*, which centered on the fate of families in the Yellow River floodplain, won the Mao Dun Literary Award. In this phase of his writing, Li Zhun sought to develop a distinctly Chinese approach to fiction by engaging with grand historical narratives. Set during the 1930s Sino-Japanese War, the novel depicts the Japanese invasion of central China and the retreat of Nationalist forces, who breached the Huayuankou Dam on the Yellow River in a desperate attempt to "use water as a weapon" against the Japanese. This catastrophic decision caused immense suffering, displacing over 10 million people across 44 counties in Henan, Jiangsu, and Anhui. Li Zhun traces the exodus through the intertwined stories of seven families, portraying their struggles with deep empathy. In the preface, Li Zhun reflects on his character portrayals: "I've tried a new approach—simply showing life as it is. 'Ten years in Yangzhou feel like a dream'—I no longer artificially elevate or diminish my characters. They are real people, each bearing flaws and the marks of tradition, not because I intended it, but because life itself is that way." He adds: "This book is titled *The Yellow River Flows East*, but it is not an elegy for bygone days. It seeks to re-evaluate, on the scales of history, the vital forces that have sustained our nation." This work, rooted in historical events and everyday realities, marks a transformation in Li Zhun's writing—a turn toward unvarnished truth and a partial liberation from the constraints of revolutionary realism.

Under Li Zhun's towering influence, Henan literature developed along his literary tradition—a path marked by both achievements and controversies. As Professor Liu Siqian notes in her literary history: "The position of 1940s-1970s Henan literature in China's literary canon remains ambiguous. Over time, critical voices have overshadowed affirmative ones—a consensus about that era's literary trends. Yet when it comes to Henan writers specifically, there's a lingering perception of opportunism (the most despised trait in Chinese literati circles), referring to their works' overt political alignment and excessive 'follow-the-tide' tendencies." However, we must acknowledge that "post-New Era local writers in Henan were directly influenced by Li Zhun, Yao Xueyin, and others to varying degrees. Li Zhun's folk sensibilities and linguistic style provided direct nourishment for a new generation—writers like Li Peifu and Zhang Yu, who, after breaking free from political constraints, made independent imagination of grassroots life their defining feature. Meanwhile, Eryue He openly acknowledged Yao Xueyin's profound impact on his work. These earlier writers left us a reference point—one that's equally open to critique—sparing later generations much trial and error."[①]

To a certain extent, Li Zhun's focus on policy directives, his exploration of national character, and his incorporation of folk resources profoundly influenced later generations of Henan writers. Zhang Yu's *Masters of the Land*, published in the November 1979 issue of *Yangtze River Literature*, was

① Liang Hong, "From 'Periphery' to 'Margins of the Center': Yan'an Literary Thought and Henan Literature from the 1940s to the 1970s," Literary Contention, no. 6, 2007.

praised by *Red Flag* magazine as "the first post-reform literary work to authentically capture peasants' aspirations toward land ownership." After Zhang Yu gained recognition, Li Zhun once took his hand and introduced him to senior literary figures, saying: "Let me tell you, this is one of our Luoyang natives—our region breeds writers." Zhang Yu never forgot another piece of advice from Li Zhun: "Zhang Yu, the language and cultural essence of Luoyang are our treasures—they're our livelihood. We must never abandon them."① Yet tradition carries its own limitations. Excessive immersion in rural narratives, depictions of village life, and the inherent power dynamics of native soil discourse often hinder the ability to capture emerging realities and new social currents. This has led to a noticeable homogenization in Henan's literary works, inevitably restricting writers from exploring broader creative dimensions.

In 2003, when asked by Liang Hong, "What do you think are the main issues facing young writers from Henan today?" Yan Lianke responded: "It's hard to say—I don't think they have any major problems. Honestly, their writing is just as strong as our generation's. If I had to pinpoint an area for improvement, it would be their collective spirit of exploration and innovation, which still feels somewhat restrained. This isn't to say every writer must experiment radically, but every writer should at least go through that process. Even if they fail, even if they ultimately return to tradition and realism, their

① Zhang Yu, "A Talented Scholar's Unrestrained Spirit," Luoyang Daily Online, September 17, 2008, accessed via: http://news.lyd.com.cn/system/2008/09/17/000509198.shtml.

understanding of those forms will be transformed—they'll achieve a conceptual leap. Overall, they are innovating, but they rarely lead the way; they often follow others. This is a question worth exploring: Why is it that, aside from Liu Zhenyun (who left Henan), Henan writers tend to take smaller, slower steps than others? Even the younger generation—this is something worth studying."[①] Since then, with the rise of Henan's "post-60s," "post-70s," and "post-80s" writers—whose upbringings and environments diverged sharply from earlier generations—their works have become more rooted in personal experience. Their engagement with tradition lacks the depth and monumental influence of their predecessors, but this shift has also opened new possibilities for literary diversity.

① Yan Lianke and Liang Hong, "The Pitfalls of the 'Central Plains Breakthrough': A Dialogue Between Yan Lianke and Liang Hong," Fiction Review, no. 1, 2003.

Chapter 3
Heavy Wings – The Many Faces of Urban Migration

The literary history of the early New Era is also a history of urban migration narratives, deeply intertwined with the restructuring of society. With the advent of the New Era, the relaxation of the hukou (household registration) system, accelerated population mobility, and the nation's expanding openness, more people than ever harbored the desire—and possibility—to move to cities. In the early years of reform and opening-up, when institutional barriers had not yet been fully dismantled, the "urban-rural dual system" strictly regulated rural migrants attempting to enter cities. During the early 1980s, two predominant narratives of urban migration emerged: the *Chen Huansheng-style* "going to town" stories and the *Gao Jialin-style* tales of educated rural youth seeking urban opportunities. By the 1990s, however, as cities became more accessible and the market economy fully took hold, "urban migration" transformed into a new, nationwide aspiration pursued relentlessly by generations.

1. The City as a Mirror

Villages emerged organically as natural extensions of human habitation, while cities developed gradually as deliberate constructs of advancing civilization. In China, the urban-rural dichotomy has been institutionally entrenched for over a millennium, tracing back to the Song Dynasty (960–1279), where cities arose not merely as population centers but as ideological counterpoints to rural existence. The "rural migrant in the city" as a novelistic discourse has traversed China's century-long modern transformation—from

Han Bangqing's 1894 Sing-Song Girls of Shanghai to the present—spanning three centuries of literary evolution. In contemporary fiction, this narrative mode has become what might be called "subaltern in appearance, yet mainstream in essence."①

Although China historically maintained a distinction between urban and rural areas, the institutionalized urban-rural dual system was not established until the late 1950s. The implementation of the Household Registration Ordinance of the People's Republic of China in 1958 marked the formalization of this uniquely Chinese system, which rigidly classified citizens into urban and rural household registrations. This legal demarcation created two mutually exclusive systems where cities and villages became closed units with severely restricted flows of production factors. Under this dual system, urban residents and peasants were accorded unequal rights and opportunities—farmers were effectively relegated to a "second-class citizen" status.②

According to sociologist Li Yining's recollections: In 1969, faculty members of Peking University were sent to work at the Liyuzhou Farm in Nanchang County, Jiangxi Province. As part of the first batch of personnel dispatched, I lived in a thatched hut by Poyang Lake for two years. During this period, I visited nearby villages and witnessed destitute peasants—often

---

① Xu Deming, "Literary Narratives of 'Rural Migrants in the City'," Literary Review, no. 1, 2005.

② Li Yining, "*On Reforming the Urban-Rural Dual System*," Journal of Peking University (Philosophy and Social Sciences Edition), no. 2, 2008.

clad in tattered clothes despite the harsh winter cold—coming to beg at our university farm. Barefoot or wearing only straw sandals, these refugees from famine stood in stark contrast to Poyang Lake's reputation as a "land of fish and rice." It was an era of deep reflection. Witnessing these scenes two decades after the founding of New China, I began questioning: Why does such extreme rural poverty persist? Could flaws in our economic system explain these contradictions? The orthodox economic theories I'd studied proved inadequate to interpret the suffering before my eyes. This intellectual crisis marked the beginning of my transformation as an economist.①

Against this social backdrop, terms like "college entrance exams," "household registration," "factory recruitment," "state employee" and "commodity grain ration" became the driving forces for rural migrants seeking to change their destinies—each phrase emblematic of 1980s China. For countless rural youth, entering the state system as an urban-registered "public employee" entitled to state-subsidized food rations represented both the ultimate goal and a badge of honor in their journey to the cities. As the writer Mo Yan once recalled, his family was overjoyed when he was promoted as an army officer—it meant he could "eat from the public rice bowl" and would never have to return to rural labor. This vividly illustrates how "rural folk" and "urbanites" inhabited separate worlds. The city's "commodity grain system",

① Li Yining, "Toward Urban-Rural Integration: Sixty Years of Institutional Transformation Since the Founding of the PRC," Journal of Peking University (Philosophy and Social Sciences Edition), no. 6, 2009.

tied to household registration, artificially constructed an "urban-rural binary" through institutionalized privileges: state-allocated food and non-staple goods, fuel supplies, job assignments, healthcare, pensions, and labor protections. Urbanites, enjoying these exclusive benefits, were effectively "a class above" rural citizens in terms of social status. This systemic inequality became the primary driving force behind educated rural youth's desperate migration to cities during this era.

Zhang Yigong's short story *Black Boy Takes a Photo*, published in the seventh issue of Shanghai Literature in 1981 and awarded the National Outstanding Short Story Prize that same year, serves as a representative work of early 1980s literature. Unlike Gao Jialin's urban migration depicted in Lu Yao's Life, the protagonist Black Boy in this story ventures to the Zhongyue Temple Fair—a temporary, constructed version of "the city." This fair embodies numerous modern urban elements: a tiger transported from the provincial zoo, funhouse mirrors from Luoyang installed in the "sacred chamber" of the temple, dozens of supply and department stores from both the local county and neighboring regions, densely packed state-run canteens, and privately owned food stalls. Together, these elements create a transient, consumerist pseudo-city that temporarily replicates urban modernity within a rural setting.

With eight yuan and forty cents earned from raising rabbits, the hardworking Black Boy arrives at the temple fair, dreaming of buying stylish clothes to emulate those young men who've become workers or have wage-earning family members. He imagines himself transformed: "Wearing a red fleece sweater under a green military-style jacket, the collar left open to flash the shiny zipper; biting the crown of a green army cap to create a crisp ridge, then tilting it low over his brow, his lively eyes darting beneath the brim. Thus, our Black Boy would embody the quintessential 1980s youth of Songshan's foothills—earning furtive, admiring glances from village girls."① When he finally spots a red fleece sweater with a small lapel and zipper—only to realize he can't afford it—he refuses to "squander" money on "a bowl of mutton soup for thirty cents or that highway-robbery noodle soup for sixty cents." Instead, he spends three yuan and eighty fen on a photograph, trading material desire for symbolic fulfillment.Black Boy's defiant internal monologue captures his pride: "So it's fine for me, Zhang Heiwa, to sweat raising angora rabbits, shearing premium 1.7-inch fibers for your foreigners' fancy 'cashmere' sweaters, but you won't serve me in return? No way! Even this American-made camera must 'click' for Zhang Heiwa—a perfectly ordinary member of the People's Republic! I'll have my moment of 'glamour,' and that's final!"② Heiwa derives immense spiritual satisfaction from having his photograph taken, a testament to rural people's yearning for a better life and their pursuit of modernity.

---

① Zhang Yigong, "*Black Boy Takes a Photo*," Shanghai Literature, no. 7, 1981.

② Zhang Yigong, *Selected Stories of Zhang Yigong*, Henan Literature and Art Publishing House, 1998, p.56.

The Photograph as a Symbol of Modernity and Disparity

The photograph, as an emblem of modern civilization, became a powerful literary device in post-reform Chinese literature, reflecting the stark urban-rural divide and the allure of consumer culture. This motif appears in seminal works of the era, often highlighting the jarring contrasts between rural livelihoods and urban modernity. For instance, Gao Xiaosheng, discussing his story *Chen Huansheng Goes to Town*, revealed: "The story draws from my own experiences. After my rehabilitation, I traveled for work and stayed in guesthouses—overnight stays cost five to eight yuan. Yet, peasants in southern Jiangsu earned just seventy to eighty fen a day. A single night's lodging consumed nearly ten days of their wages. How could human labor be so cheap, while a bed could be so expensive? Even ordinary cadres and workers earned only sixty to seventy yuan monthly—three combined salaries barely matched the price of a hotel bed. Peasants couldn't fathom this disparity; when told, they'd laugh, thinking I was spinning tall tales."① Similarly, Tie Ning's *Oh, Xiangxue* depicts a stationery box—imbued with urban sophistication—that captivates the rural protagonist, symbolizing unattainable modernity. In Lu Yao's *Life*, Gao Jialin's fascination with the city library mirrors this theme, framing urban spaces as gateways to knowledge and broader horizons.

---

① Gao Xiaosheng Literary Research Association (ed.), *Gao Xiaosheng: Critical Essays and Studies*, Jiangsu Literature and Art Publishing House, 2014, p.334.

In *Black Boy Takes a Photo*, the photograph itself becomes a vessel of modernity and aspiration. The image captures Black Boy transformed: "Handsome, prosperous, and radiant, with a dignified posture, a mocking glint in his eyes, and a captivating smile—as if he were attending a cocktail party on some grand diplomatic mission." Yet the backdrop remains the Tianzhong Pavilion of Zhongyue Temple, its red walls and green tiles, carved beams and painted rafters, steeped in antiquity. Through this photographic act, Black Boy achieves a symbolic ascent from rural to urban, even fantasizing about calling the United States... Clutching the photo to his chest, he feels a surge of satisfaction and exhilaration. He imagines his mother's joy, for what he brings home is not just an image but "a kaleidoscope of aspirations, proof that Black Boy can 'eat well and dress well.'" According to Lacan's mirror stage theory, "the subject anticipates, through illusion, the maturation of its bodily unity by projecting itself onto an external object—a constitutive process that binds the 'I' to this object through manifold fantasies." Furthermore, "this mechanism integrates individual formation into historical becoming, enabling the 'ego' to negotiate complex cultural contingencies within society."① In the dynamic interplay between posing, capturing, and viewing, Black Boy completes a psychological leap from village to city—a mediated flight enabled by the camera's alchemy.

① Wang Yuechuan, *A Coursebook on Contemporary Western Literary Theory*, Fudan University Press, 2008, p.57.

2. "The City's Light" and the Relentless Urban Migrants

Li Peifu, as one of Henan's earliest writers to focus on rural-to-urban migration narratives, began crafting a series of works on this theme in the 1990s, including *The Golden House*, *City White Paper*, and *The City's Light*. In his writing, the city emerges as a dominant force—both alluring and oppressive—while the migrants themselves are portrayed with an almost existential relentlessness, severing ties to their rural pasts with startling determination. A prime example is the story of the "New Mother" in *City White Paper*:

She found Pang Qiugui in the courtyard of the county education bureau. By the time she located him, night had fallen, and in the darkness, her large eyes shone like lamps—it was by the light of those eyes that she made her way to Pang Qiugui's dormitory. That night, she stayed in his single-room dormitory... and thus, she willingly became his wife. She remained his wife for four years and seven days—two years unofficially, and two years and seven days officially. During her time as Pang Qiugui's wife, whether formal or informal, she twice bravely "eliminated" two small masses of flesh, two fragile lives. And then, clutching her newly acquired urban household registration, she strode confidently, radiant and self-assured, toward another city.[①]

① Li Peifu, *City White Paper*, Shaanxi Normal University Press, 2000, p.14.

A rural woman, driven solely by her yearning for the city, resorts to selling her body and even killing her unborn child as she relentlessly pursues urban life. Such extreme actions—lacking sufficient motivational foundation—ultimately undermine the narrative's coherence and completeness. This reflects Li Peifu's prevailing creative temperament during this period. As a writer, Li Peifu keenly recognized the irreversibility of rural-to-urban migration early on. Yet within the cognitive framework of that era, the city loomed as a black hole—a gravitational force that drew people in only to annihilate their humanity. This same relentless logic of urbanization unfolds in *The City's Light*, where the protagonist's desperate bid for urban belonging similarly culminates in existential erasure.

The title *The City's Light* is strikingly direct, embodying boundless yearning and desire. For Feng Jiachang, a rural youth, his first life goal is to wear a "four-pocket" jacket—a sartorial symbol of cadreship. "Putting on the 'four pockets' means entering the ranks of state cadres, becoming 'one of the nation's people.' But what is 'the nation'? It's a ticket to the city, a ladder of bureaucratic ranks, an all-encompassing system of entitlements..."[①] To secure his urban future, Feng abandons Liu Hanxiang, his devoted fiancée who waited faithfully for him for five years, and instead marries a woman with urban connections. Yet, in the city's glare, everything is laid bare: "Under the lights, it was all naked flesh—mad, writhing flesh, like a city stripped of

① Li Peifu, *The City's Lights*, Changjiang Literature & Art Press, 2003, p.51.

its pretenses. The city's nobility, its restraint, its hardness, its sanctimoniousness—all dissolved in an instant into a raging flood..." In the end, Feng Jiachang is left with an inexplicable sense of defeat. "He couldn't even say whether he had conquered the 'city' or if the 'city' had raped him... One thing was clear: he had entered the city, but at the cost of his dignity."①

Though he endlessly longed for "the scent of hay and the musk of youth, mingling in a makeshift hut like a pot of meat-cooked rice! That happiness was steeped in animal warmth, in dizzy recklessness, in the thrilling fear of abandon. How lush it was—how utterly, achingly 'astonishing.'"② But he could not suppress his frenzied desire for the city. He even schemed relentlessly to drag his younger brothers into urban life alongside him. The novel is regarded as "a spiritual chronicle of peasants' migration from countryside to city, framed in grand historical perspective."③ Here, city and village stand as stark opposites: the city embodies civilization, modernity, and wealth; the village represents idealism, pastoral nostalgia, and poverty. And so, more and more choose to abandon everything for the city—clawing for roots in concrete, even as the soil of their past clings stubbornly to their souls.

The relentless pursuit of urban life was inextricably linked to rural poverty in post-1949 China. Statistical surveys of urban and household incomes

---

① Li Peifu, *The City's Lights*, Changjiang Literature & Art Press, 2003, pp.191-192.

② Ibid., p.45.

③ He Hong, "*The Tenacious Explorer and Profound Thinker*," Fiction Review, no. 2 (2013).

reveal stark disparities between workers and peasants in both consumption and income over decades. In 1957, the per capita consumption expenditure was 205 yuan for urban workers versus 79 yuan for peasants—a 1:2.59 ratio. By 1980, this gap widened to 477 yuan (urban) versus 168 yuan (rural), a 1:2.84 ratio. Income disparities followed a similar trajectory: in 1964, urban annual income averaged 243 yuan, rising to 514 yuan by 1980, while rural income grew from 102 yuan to 194 yuan—widening from 1:2.4 to 1:2.7. The gaps in education, healthcare, and cultural life were even more pronounced. In healthcare, in 1980, rural areas had only 0.8 doctors per 1,000 people—no improvement since 1957—while cities increased from 1.3 to 3.2 doctors, expanding the urban-rural disparity from 1:1.7 to 1:4.2. In cultural access, rural areas had one film screening team per 11,000 people, compared to 510 cinema seats per 10,000 urban residents. County-level performing arts troupes served one rural audience per 350,000 people, while urbanites attended 4.4 performances annually versus peasants' 0.6.

Rural poverty left an entire generation with indelible memories of suffering and humiliation. As writer Yan Lianke recalled of his youth in the 1970s: "What defined that era for me wasn't revolution—it was hunger and endless labor. As a child, I watched educated urban youth who never worked the fields, strolling through the village in clean clothes, playing flutes. Slowly, I understood: we peasants were born lowly, while they were celestial beings. I didn't resent their urban origins; I just quietly lamented my own birth in this dirt."[①] Li Peifu, reflecting on *The City's Light*, stated: "This novel is about escape—breaking free from the land, from the village. It's a rebellion fueled by longing for the city's glow."[②]

For Feng Jiachang, the countryside was a landscape of poverty and isolation.

In Shangliang village, the Feng family stood alone—"like a single stalk of sorghum towering over a field of millet, utterly solitary."

His father was known only as "Old Brother-in-Law", a title reserved for live-in sons-in-law across the Central Plains. The epithet, laced with mockery beneath its surface courtesy, marked him as an outsider—"a branch grafted onto another family's tree," forever distanced by blood and belonging.[③]

As Fei Xiaotong observed in *From the Soil*, "The fundamental structure of Chinese rural society is what I call a 'differential mode of association', a web woven from personal connections." For those with the "wrong" surname, like Feng's father, this web offered no foothold. After their mother's death, the brothers went barefoot even in snow—"they stepped out shoeless into that endless white." It was then that Feng glimpsed a pair of "tennis shoes" on a visiting urban relative: pristine white, with "bouncy soles and nylon

---

① Yan Lianke, *My Father's Generation*, Yunnan People's Publishing House, 2009, p.27.

② Sun Jing, "An Intellectual's Examination of Conscience: Interview with Writer Li Peifu," Literary Gazette, April 2, 2012.

③ Li Peifu, *The City's Lights*, Changjiang Literature & Art Press, 2003, p.7.

socks." At that moment, he vowed with solemn clarity: "We will have shoes." These experiences hardened Feng Jiachang's resolve to never return to the countryside. Faced with his brothers' desperate pleas, he declared with cold finality:

"Listen—I won't go back. Soon, you'll all leave too. Everyone of you will become city men. This is my mission now, the Feng family's great cause. The rest... can't be helped. Yes, we owe her a debt. Let the curses fall on me alone. I do this for our family's future..."①

The author critiques Feng's moral abandonment—his trade of conscience for ambition—even while offering "empathetic understanding" of his transformation. Yet alongside this grim pragmatism, Li Peifu crafts an idealistic counterpoint: Liu Hanxiang. Betrayed, she neither seeks revenge nor flees, but remains on the city's fringe as "Fragrant Auntie," cultivating flowers. Li later reflected: "This novel holds two plains-born fairytales: one chasing a material 'city,' the other building a spiritual one. Though differing in scope, both succeed in their own ways."② Fragrant Auntie's moral force quietly redeems others. The Feng brothers achieve brutal success—"The Feng clan completes its great migration! The four brothers and their descendants now hold proper urban residency (in major cities), bear dignified city names,

① Li Peifu, *The City's Lights*, Changjiang Literature & Art Press, 2003, p.207.

② Zhou Baiyi and Qin Wenzhong, "*Li Peifu Ignites 'City Lights' with Passion: A Dialogue on the Novel and Its Author,*" People's Daily (Overseas Edition), April 22, 2003.

and have fully evolved from grass-eaters to meat-eaters (their children drink milk from birth)."[①] Yet before her grave, "their legs buckle—one by one, they kneel."

Li Peifu later reflected on the psychological drivers behind his ruthless urban migrants during this creative period: "In recent years, my perspective has shifted. I once believed money to be the root of all evil—but I was wrong. Poverty, especially spiritual poverty, inflicts far greater damage on a person's life than wealth ever could. In this regard, Feng Jiachang is profoundly emblematic."[②] This insight allows us to grasp Feng's relentless drive—his willingness to bear condemnation for abandoning rural life. His actions embody the fracturing of society under the pressure of China's uneven development: cities surging forward while villages stagnate.

In traditional agrarian societies, as Fei Xiaotong observed in *From the Soil*, "rural communities are deeply rooted in the land—people live, grow, and die where they were born. Not only is population mobility minimal, but the land itself remains largely unchanged. In this timeless environment, individuals rely not only on their own experience but also on the accumulated wisdom of ancestors. A farmer's life revolves solely around the cyclical turn of seasons, not epochal shifts. Solutions to life's problems are inherited, not

---

① Li Peifu, *The City's Lights*, Changjiang Literature & Art Press, 2003, pp.402-403.

② Sun Jing, "An Intellectual's Examination of Conscience: Interview with Writer Li Peifu," Literary Gazette, April 2, 2012.

invented. The more a practice has been validated by generations past, the more fiercely it is preserved. Thus, 'quoting Yao and Shun' becomes a way of life—nostalgia functions as survival insurance." Against this backdrop of rural stagnation—where poverty and inertia reign—the vibrant, kaleidoscopic city exerts an almost fatal allure. For both Feng Jiachang and Gao Jialin, urban women represent not just romantic partners but conquerable territory—a gateway to the city and a requisite element for "claiming" urban space. It is precisely this perception that drives their moral deformation, leading them to abandon their rural fiancées in pursuit of ambition and desire.

Raymond Williams' analysis of rural and urban dichotomies offers a framework to understand these tensions: "The country has been conceived as a natural way of life: peace, innocence, and simple virtue. The city, by contrast, is seen as a center of achievement: learning, communication. Yet strong negative associations also emerge—the city as noise, worldliness, and ambition; the countryside as backwardness, ignorance, and limitation."[①] This theoretical lens illuminates Li Peifu's and Lu Yao's novels: In *The City's Light*, Feng Jiachang's moral betrayal and psychological distortion in his ruthless urban pursuit contrast sharply with Fragrant Auntie's embodiment of rural virtues like benevolence and integrity. Similarly, in *Life*, Gao Jialin's abandonment of Qiaozhen stems from his yearning for the city's promise, despite

① Raymond Williams, *The Country and the City*, trans. Han Ziman, Liu Ge, and Xu Shanshan, The Commercial Press, 2013, p.1.

its moral ambiguities. Yet whether romanticizing pastoral nostalgia or surrendering to urban ambition, escaping the countryside became a generational destiny. This dualistic perception of the city has fundamentally shaped post-reform narratives of rural-to-urban migration, leaving them suspended between the consumerist city and the productive city. On one hand, the interplay of personal rural memory and socialist ideological conditioning frames urban spaces as "realms of sin" in migrant imaginations. On the other hand, the city's material allure and its role as the vanguard of national industrialization constantly erase these moral stigmas.[①] This duality evokes in readers both moral repulsion toward the relentless compromises depicted in these urban migration narratives, yet also an inescapable empathy

3. The Story Beyond the Story

While urban literature flourished, the personal narratives of writers themselves mirrored the broader migration to cities. As China's urbanization unfolded, generation after generation was swept into this transformative tide. Just as literary themes shifted toward urban life and works themselves "entered the city," writers too embarked on their own mass migration to metropolitan centers. This marked a stark departure from the tradition of the "Seventeen-Year Literature" period (1949–1966), exemplified by Liu Qing, who left the city to immerse himself in rural Huangpu Village for over a decade,

① Xu Gang, "'Rural-to-Urban Migration' in 'Seventeen-Year Literature' (1949-1966)," Literary Contention, no. 8 (2012).

producing the epic *The Builders*, a chronicle of collectivization. In contrast, the post-Reform era saw writers increasingly flocking to cities, becoming integral participants in urban life rather than observers from afar.

For Henan writers, migration to cities typically followed several paths: college entrance exams, military service, factory recruitment, or literary success. Among those who entered through higher education, Liu Zhenyun and Li Er stand as emblematic figures. Liu Zhenyun, seizing the opportunity after the reinstatement of the Gaokao, gained admission to Peking University's Chinese Department in 1978. After graduating in 1982, he joined *Farmer's Daily*. His novella *Tower Hamlet* revisits his own struggles after military demobilization—failing to secure an officer's rank, enduring hardship, and eventually preparing for university exams through relentless effort. "I returned home after my military service. As my father put it, I'd wasted four years: no Party membership, no promotion—just a thicker beard to show for it." "Winter came. The classroom leaked cold air; the dormitory leaked cold air. There was no refuge from the chill. Then it snowed, and the ice that followed made nights unbearable. I'd wake up frozen at midnight." "Wang Quan's eldest child brought him steamed buns again. Clutching the boy's dark-skinned hand, Wang sighed: 'When Dad passes the exams and becomes an official, you and your mother will taste a better life!'" "I knew I'd done well. I sensed I'd be admitted—if not to a top-tier university, then at least a decent one. When I told my father, who'd waited outside the exam site for two days, he was speechless. For the first time in his life, this old peasant hugged me like a Westerner, murmuring in disbelief: 'How can this be? How can this be? " The crushing poverty of rural life drove many to stake everything on the Gaokao. In that era, its reinstatement represented the rare chance to alter one's fate through sheer effort—not connections or luck.

Zhou Daxin and Yan Lianke, among others, escaped rural life through military service. In later essays, Zhou reflected on his journey out of the Central Plains:

"The village elders drilled it into me: 'Boy, only by passing the college exams can you become an official. Only as an official can you eat fragrant and drink spicy [live luxuriously]. Only then can your parents taste happiness.' So I resolved to study my way into power. I became obsessed—ranking top in every class, serving as academic monitor. Winter mornings, I walked six li to school before dawn, lighting kerosene lamps to study. Summer downpours soaked through my straw raincloak, but I'd wring out my clothes and endure. Then the Cultural Revolution erupted during middle school, snapping my university dreams mid-stride."[①]

In 1970, at eighteen, "I boarded an eastbound military freight train, watching the Central Plains recede through the slatted door—my heart held faint traces of nostalgia, but mostly swelled with exhilaration. 'At last,' I

---

① Zhou Daxin, *Eighteen Years Rooted in the Central Plains*, China Literature and History Press, 2012, p.5.

thought, 'I can venture into the world on my own...'"①

For Zhou Daxin, the interruption of the college entrance examination due to the "Cultural Revolution" rendered his efforts futile, while an unexpected opportunity to enlist in the military became a turning point that changed his destiny. Similarly, for Yan Lianke, how to escape the impoverished rural life was a persistent concern that weighed on his mind during his youth. After failing the college entrance exam, Yan Lianke also found an opportunity by joining the military. Yet staying in the army—and by extension, in the city—posed new challenges. His essay "*The Reading That Changed My Fate*" recounts his youthful struggle to escape rural life and break free from the land that bound him.

Back then—nearly thirty years ago in the mid-1970s—society resembled the biogas pit at my village's edge: fetid and chaotic. For me, a rural teenager, the grandest dream was to escape the countryside after high school, to flee the land forever, and find in the city that most sacred of privileges: a job where I could collect wages by signing my name each month.

The Dividing Line is a novel whose binding appears rather plain and dated by today's standards. However, its synopsis contains one notable line (or idea): Zhang Kangkang, a sent-down youth who had been relocated to the Great Northern Wilderness, was transferred to work in the provincial capital,

① Ibid., p.6.

Harbin, through the process of writing and revising this novel.

So—writing a novel could move someone from the the Great Northern Wilderness to Harbin, the bustling provincial capital. So—writing could change people's fate, redirect the course of their lives.

And so, before I even graduated high school, I secretly began teaching myself to write fiction. I began treating reading like panning for gold. And in truth, just as writing altered Zhang Kangkang's destiny, every shift in my own life became inextricably tied to the act of writing.①

Fellow "50s generation" writer Zhang Yu entered Luoyang city in 1970 through factory recruitment, where he later discovered the literary world at his workplace. Through writing, he eventually moved to the provincial capital as a professional writer. Zhang Yu views himself as "a product of reform and opening-up—without it, there would be no me." He summarizes the policy's impact on his creative work as "intellectual liberation and education, nourishment for life and culture." "Without reform and opening-up, how could a peasant's child like me have become a writer?" Zhang elaborates: "In China's cultural history, reform and opening-up was a monumental ideological movement that dramatically overturned traditional thinking and comprehensively connected us with world culture. Without it, peasant children like us might never have entered cities—or if we did, we'd have been stuck rigidly

---

① Yan Lianke, "*Reading That Changes Fate*", in *Yan Lianke's Critical Essays*, Kunming: Yunnan People's Publishing House, 2013, pp. 93–94.

factory-bound, incapable of spiritual pursuits, let alone writing fiction."[①] For decades, "urbanites" and "country folk" seemed like entirely separate species. As Mo Yan recalled in an interview about his military promotion: "I was more thrilled than when winning the Nobel Prize. I felt reborn—no longer a peasant destined to 'face the yellow earth under the sky.' Now I was an officer with cadre status. Even if discharged, I'd become a local government clerk. My father was overjoyed—for a family like ours, having a son become an officer was historic. We could finally walk tall in the village."

It can be said that due to shared social and historical circumstances, this generation carried remarkably similar life trajectories. The famine and poverty of their rural childhoods and adolescence left indelible scars and memories, while the desperate urge to escape the countryside and the exhilaration of urban arrival became defining forces during their transitional years. Yet as time passed, they discovered they could never fully shake off the shackles of their rural roots. To them, their hometown remained like an inescapable shadow—a long tail that trailed behind no matter how far they ran. Even after two decades in the city, their writing still clung to rural sentiment: "I am a kite let loose from the countryside into the city, drifting for twenty years, yet the string remains tied to my family's roof beam. In the city, I've learned to tuck my tail between my legs—twenty years later, I still haven't rid myself of that sweet potato stench. I paste paper-flower smiles on my face, say 'hello'

---

① Zhang Yu: *The Unrestrained Spirit of a Talented Scholar*, http://lywb.lyd.com.cn/html/2008-09/17/content_442870.htm?sn=_X_

and 'thank you,' but deep in my bones, I know I'm still just a country bumpkin."[1]

"Modern society is not composed of neatly layered groups with clear boundaries, but of individuals who simultaneously inhabit multiple roles and reference points. Depending on social conditions and historical contexts, they draw from personal or collective past experiences to choose different forms of reference and identity."

"Modern society is not composed of neatly stratified groups with clear boundaries, but rather of individuals who simultaneously assume multiple roles and reference points. Depending on social conditions and historical circumstances, they select different forms of reference and identity based on their personal or collective past experiences."[2] Therefore, in the works of this generation of writers, the predominant urban characters often possess rural backgrounds, with their familiar domains largely rooted in rural life. Consequently, their writings frequently exhibit intersections of urban and rural elements, along with spatial transitions between these settings. As Lu Yao once remarked: "What I know best is the 'borderland' between village and city—I lived there long and still shuttle between these realms. I've said I un-

---

① Zhang Yu, "Rural Sentiments", in Urban Free Roaming: A Self-Selected Collection of Zhang Yu's Novellas and Short Stories, Beijing: Huaxia Publishing House, 1997, p. 221.

② (FR) Alfred Grosser, *Le Dilemme de l'Identité* [*The Dilemma of Identity*], trans. Wang Kun, Beijing: Social Sciences Academic Press, 2010, pp. 3-4.

derstand those who smell of both soil and asphalt, and the urbanites and villagers linked to such people."[①] Indeed, these writers embodied the Gao Jialins and Sun Shaopings of their era—educated youths of the 1970s–80s who were educated but lacked the luck to enter university or secure jobs, thus seeming disqualified from society's mainstream currents. Yet they refused to be confined to narrow lives. Instead, they waged desperate battles on the hardest paths—too busy improving their material conditions to pontificate on human fate, yet never abandoning spiritual pursuits. They neither scorned mundane existence nor stopped probing life's depths..."[②] Their stories chronicle both the grit required to escape rural hardship and the emotional toll of that ascent—a duality etched into literature by those who lived it.

In contrast, the slightly younger "post-60s" and "post-70s" writers, having grown up in less harsh environments, lack such stark psychological contrasts in their urban narratives. Their works tend to focus more on the mental states of urban dwellers: Shao Li's novel *My Quality of Life* traces Wang Qilong's journey—from rural poverty to urban academia through the Gaokao, burdened by his grandmother's hopes yet haunted by his peasant origins. His struggle for dignity unfolds alongside questions of what "quality of life" truly means in this ascent. The novella *Minghui's Christmas* depicts a proud rural girl who, after failing college exams, becomes a sex worker in the city rather

---

① Lu Yao, *Collected Works of Lu Yao (Vol. 2)*, Xi'an: Shaanxi People's Publishing House, 1993, p. 401.

② Lu Yao, *Ordinary World*, Beijing: Writer's Publishing House, 2005, p. 272.

than face ridicule. Her doomed fantasy of urban belonging ends in suicide when reality shatters her dreams. Qiao Ye's *I Truly Love You* and *The Confession* delve into urban drifters' emotional crises, layered with broader social-historical reflections. Xi Tongfa's novella collection *Sparrow Dialogues* captures the existential wandering of city nomads. Li Qingyuan's *Su Rang's Redemption* dissects urban spiritual displacement: the protagonist's college romance with a literature department beauty collapses post-graduation when she chooses material security. Forced by rent pressures to share a flat with the unattractive Xie Chunli, Su Rang descends into exploitation—using "not loving her" to justify cruelty. Later, he becomes entangled in his rural father's disputes, achieves self-redemption by resolving the conflict, finds his place, and begins an ordinary life with Xie Chunli—a narrative that also addresses the spiritual anchoring of urban dwellers.

Of course, these literary works are constructed against the backdrop of accelerating urbanization. "In the last two decades of the 20th century, as China's modernization accelerated, Henan Province finally embarked on urban development. The modernization of Henan, driven by urbanization, presented a vibrant new outlook. Jiyuan County became Jiyuan City, Ruyang County turned into Ruzhou City, Dengfeng County transformed into Dengfeng City, and Gong County evolved into Gongyi City. Mixian County became Xinmi City, Deng County became Dengzhou City, Yu County became Yuzhou City... The number of cities in the province increased from 13 in 1949 to 38."[①] Urbanization and modernization are not merely about paving roads and erecting skyscrapers. At a deeper level, they signify a transformation in societal values and behavioral norms, reflecting a shift in the cultural psyche of its members.

For the younger "post-80s" and "post-90s" writers, the rise of cities, the advent of globalization, the ubiquity of digital connectivity, and their own urban upbringings have enabled them to capture metropolitan life with greater fluency, focusing on urbanites' existential states while softening the historical tension between city and countryside. As Beijing-raised "post-80s" writer Huo Yan observes: "Writers of the 1950s clung to rural nostalgia even when living in cities. I can only write the city instinctively—what they fled is what sustains me. I can't imagine life beyond these concrete walls; cold and impersonal as they are, they've never felt monstrous."[②] Henan writers like Nan Feiyan, Chen Hongwei, and Wang Xiaopeng exemplify this shift. Their works shed the rural undertones of earlier generations, zeroing in instead on urban lives and fates, free from the old rural-urban dialectic.

---

① Lu Shuyuan, "Gazing at Henan: An Experiment in Visualized Writing", in *Spiritual Central Plains: 20th-Century Henan Literature*, Kaifeng: Henan University Press, 2002, p. 89.

② Huo Yan, "*How I Came to Know Myself*", in October No. 4, 2013.

Chapter 4
The Many Faces of Cities and People – Life and Survival Under the Lens of Modernity

Since the 1990s, literature centered on urban life has proliferated in China. As scholar Wang Binbin notes, "Before 1949, 'urban literature' had established its own tradition... but this lineage was interrupted after 1949." It was only in the 1990s that works truly capturing contemporary city life emerged in significant numbers, "finally reviving the pre-1949 urban literary tradition."① This resurgence coincided with a mass migration—people of diverse habits and backgrounds abandoning rural roots for cities, especially metropolises—a phenomenon emblematic of economic growth and social progress. Whether in the East or the West, the history of cities has always been intertwined with the history of civilization. Through these urban narratives, writers have unveiled the many faces of China's modernization.

1. Starting with A Lifeline of Chicken Feathers

In the late 1980s and early 1990s, Henan-born writer Liu Zhenyun published *The Unit* (a novella in *Beijing Literature*, Issue 2, 1989) and *A Lifeline of Chicken Feathers* (a novella in *The Storyteller*, Issue 1, 1991), which became seminal works of the "New Realism" movement and marked a defining voice of 1990s literature. The story opens with a simple yet telling detail: the souring of tofu in Xiao Lin's home. Both Xiao Lin and Xiao Li are university graduates who once brimmed with poetic idealism and grand ambitions. Yet, after just a few years in the real world, Xiao Li transforms from a quiet,

① Wang Binbin, "The Death and Rebirth of 'Urban Literature': From 'Between Our Couple' to 'The Gourmet'", in Fiction Review No. 5, 2003.

dreamy young woman into a disheveled, nagging housewife who masters the art of stealing water by dripping the faucet overnight. Her world narrows to the mundane rhythms of daily survival—buying tofu, commuting to work, eating, sleeping, doing laundry, and managing the nanny and child. Lofty aspirations and career ideals? All vanished like smoke. Xiao Lin's life follows a similar trajectory. The narrative unfolds through the flow of daily trivialities—small, repetitive, and suffocating.

Director Feng Xiaogang, who adapted *A Lifeline of Chicken Feathers* into a TV series, once remarked on the work's deeper implications. He noted that while Liu Zhenyun's narrative focuses on the mundane—daily routines, familial squabbles, workplace drudgery—it is far from a mere chronicle of trivialities. Beneath the surface, the story grapples with the tension between the "grand" and the "petty"—what history deems significant versus what truly shapes ordinary lives. To underscore this theme, Feng deliberately opened the series with a montage of monumental global events: the collapse of the Soviet Union, Mandela's election, Clinton's presidency, African refugee crises—images of undisputed historical weight. Yet, as he observed, "For someone like Xiao Lin, these 'epochal' events pale beside the immediacy of securing housing, enrolling a child in daycare, or transferring a spouse's job. To ordinary people, life's 'big' questions are measured in centimeters, not kilometers."[①]

In this sense, *A Lifeline of Chicken Feathers* takes on a deeper symbolic weight—it marks the dissolution of 1980s grand narratives and idealism. The 1980s are often romanticized as literature's golden age, when "writers and literature shouldered the burden of speaking for the nation, of collective reflection; it was an era of grand storytelling, where authors and narrators stood apart, united in a chorus of national reckoning. In the rush to champion humanism and individuality, writers never truly 'found' themselves—the so-called 'self' remained obscured beneath collective narration. This paradox, absurd as it sounds, defined the 1980s."[②] Thus, symbolically, Liu Zhenyun's *A Lifeline of Chicken Feathers* fired the opening shot of the 1990s. The phrase "a lifeline of chicken feathers" itself became an apt, bone-deep summation of the decade: time dissolved into the mundane, life reduced to the people and events we encounter daily—all as weightless and chaotic as scattered feathers. The novel begins with "everything triggered by a spoiled block of tofu" and ends with the protagonist, Xiao Lin, queuing up the next morning to buy more. This circular futility reveals a sobering truth: every era has its own version of the same day. The 1980s were a time of reflection, yet brimming with hope and rebirth; the 1990s? Just another day buying tofu, life

---

① Feng Xiaogang & Tao Dongfeng, "Seeking Common Ground Between Audience Psychology and Artistic Taste: A Dialogue Between Feng Xiaogang and Tao Dongfeng", in Southern Cultural Forum No. 6, 1997.

② Jing Wendong, "Chasing the 1990s: Six Question Marks on the Fiction Writing of the Decade", Fiction Review No. 1, 1998.

dictated by its perishability.[①]

The author also appears to deliberately contrast the earlier idealistic sentiments with the mundane realities of present life, prominently featuring a once-literary poet nicknamed “Little Li Bai” in vivid detail.

“Little Li Bai” was Xiaolin’s university classmate. Back in their school days, the two were close friends, both passionate about poetry and joined the campus literary society together. At that time, everyone spoke of striving, brimming with an indomitable pioneering spirit. “Little Li Bai” was immensely talented and diligent, writing an average of three poems a day. His works, bold and unrestrained—spanning five thousand years of history, effortlessly invoking emperors like Qin Shi Huang, Han Wudi, Tang Taizong, and Song Taizu—were even published in some newspapers and magazines, earning him the nickname “Little Li Bai.” He attracted flocks of female admirers. Yet after graduation, everyone scattered like smoke in the wind.

This unexpected reunion took place right in front of “Little Li Bai’s” street stall. Faced with Xiaolin’s question—”Do you still write poetry?”—”Little Li Bai” replied: “That was just youthful folly! What’s poetry? Poetry is pretentious, frivolous nonsense! If I still wrote poems now, I’d starve to death! Just scraping by.” He scoffed, “Still talking about poetry? Bullshit! I’ve seen through it all—no more wild fantasies, no more dreams of

① Jing Wendong: Chasing the Nineties—Six Question Marks on 1990s Fiction Writing. Fiction Review, No. 1, 1998.

standing out. Just blend into the crowd, think about nothing—that's the most comfortable way to live." After their conversation, Xiaolin quickly came to terms with reality. He began helping "Little Li Bai" sell ducks after work, earning 20 yuan a day. *"Made 180 in nine days—bought my wife a trench coat and my daughter a five-jin Hami melon. Everyone was all smiles."* Ideals and mundanity had swiftly traded places.

Marshall Berman argues: "Today, men and women across the world share a crucial kind of experience—an experience of time and space, of the self and others, of life's possibilities and perils. I propose to call this experience 'modernity.' To be modern is to find ourselves in an environment that promises us adventure, power, joy, growth, transformation of ourselves and the world—and, at the same time, that threatens to destroy everything we have, everything we know, everything we are... To be modern is to be part of a universe in which, as Marx said, 'all that is solid melts into air.'" ①

Thus, for Xiaolin, compared to the tangible reality of money, "face and criticism truly amount to nothing." The daily 20 yuan earned from helping Little Li Bai with his duck stall was far more important than preserving dignity. Meanwhile, even his hometown had become a burden to him. His elementary school teacher—who had once shown him kindness—came to Beijing for medical treatment and stopped by to visit, bringing two jars of sesame

① (US) Marshall Berman: *All That Is Solid Melts into Air: The Experience of Modernity*, translated by Xu Dajian and Zhang Ji, The Commercial Press, 2003, p.15.

oil as a gift. Yet Xiaolin found himself unable to offer any real assistance in return. After the teacher left, Xiaolin stood watching the receding bus, tears streaming uncontrollably down his face. The next day, while reading the newspaper at the office, he came across an article about a high-ranking official who had revered his teachers throughout his life—how he had brought his two surviving childhood mentors to Beijing, housed them in the finest accommodations, and shown them around the entire city. Unable to contain himself, Xiaolin blurted out: "Who wouldn't want to honor their teachers? I'd love to put my teacher up in the best place and show him around Beijing too—if only I had the means!"

This work marks a departure from the previous heroic writing tendencies, shifting its focus to the fate of ordinary people—reflecting, to some extent, society's broader transition from grand narratives to everyday life. In the 1980s, the older generation of writers concerned themselves with reform, China's future direction, the suffering of the people, and historical reflection. For Liu Zhenyun, young writers were expected to follow in their predecessors' footsteps, burdened by the weight of such heavy themes that "the pen felt too heavy to lift." "Every day, I agonized over how to address reform, how to reflect on history, how to ponder China's path forward—until eventually, I grew sick of writing. If literature had to be written this way, it held no joy for me whatsoever."① The writing of *Tower Hamlet*, *The Unit*, and *A*

---

① Xu Mei and Liu Zhenyun: "*Who Will Accompany Me to Bianliang?*" in Southern People Weekly, No. 30, 2007.

Wilderness of Feathers also mirrors Liu Zhenyun's own life journey—leaving military service, taking the college entrance exam, moving to the city, and settling into urban employment. This personal connection lends his works an exceptional warmth, vividness, and attention to detail.

2. My Quality of Life and I Truly Love You

The momentum of reform and opening-up was accompanied by vigorous urban construction. Due to the stagnation of the pre-revolution era, China's modern urbanization process did not officially begin until the 1980s—nearly a century and a half behind the West, where large-scale modern urbanization had been underway since the 19th century. The Reform and Opening-Up Policy injected new vitality into China and created fresh opportunities for urban development, propelling Chinese cities onto a rapid growth trajectory. Since the 1980s, China's urban expansion has progressed at an extraordinary pace, with particularly dramatic transformations occurring after the 1990s. "In 1990, China had only 467 cities, but by 1995 this number had increased to 640, reaching 668 by 1999—an astonishing growth rate of dozens of cities annually. Meanwhile, the urban population surged from 118.25 million in 1990 to 230 million in 1999."①

Since the 1990s, urban literature has garnered increasing attention from

① Xie Ranhao: "*How Should We Approach Urbanization?*", Economic Daily, April 2, 2003.

writers and scholars. In the first issue of *Shanghai Literature* (1995), the journal published an "*Announcement for the 'New Urban Fiction Series' Contest and Awards*," which proclaimed: "Cities are becoming the most significant cultural landscape of 1990s China. A new urban citizenry—distinct from the planned-economy era—has quietly emerged and begun to assume leading roles. In the secular pursuit of prosperity and moderate wealth, individual vitality surges unprecedentedly, yet remains primal and crude. Urban development will become a focal point of contemporary Chinese culture. What it ultimately brings to this ancient civilization remains uncertain, but it has already become an inescapable cultural question of our time... 'New Urban Fiction' should emphasize portraying our era, exploring and expressing today's cities, citizens, and the evolving value systems." The vitality of individuals and the meaning of growth have emerged as new questions. Cities witnessed an influx of migrants from other regions, and their living conditions and psychological states increasingly became a focus of literary attention.

Shao Li's novel *My Quality of Life* (People's Literature Publishing House, 2004) serves as a representative work. The story chronicles the struggles of Wang Qilong, a young man who migrates from the countryside to the city. The author deliberately begins with a prologue about Wang's grandmother—a refined urban woman from an elite family who, after suffering wartime humiliation, was forced into rural exile. Investing all her hopes in Wang Qilong, the grandmother raised him personally, imparting her values through both instruction and example while vigilantly guarding against his adoption of rural habits. Her singular ambition was to see him escape the countryside for urban life. Though Wang Qilong fulfills this expectation by gaining admission to a prestigious university—a potential turning point—the city fails to embrace him. His urban journey begins under the weight of profound alienation.

Wang Qilong wore the white shirt and navy twill trousers his grandmother had sewn for him—garments long envied by village children—with every button fastened tightly at the collar and cuffs. On his feet were the black corduroy cloth shoes with layered soles, painstakingly made by his mother who had gone to great lengths to borrow shoe patterns for them. When he set off from home carrying his luggage, the entire village came out to watch. Their gazes of admiration settled upon him like sunlight. He felt utterly self-assured, his strides so measured and effortless that he might have been described as "light as a swallow." Now his grandmother could stand before the crowd, watching him with serene pride—an artist beholding her masterpiece. Now, standing in the registration line at his Wuhan university, Wang Qilong watched his new classmates gliding through campus like fish—vibrant in their patterned short-sleeves and wide-leg trousers, their leather shoes gleaming. For the first time in his twenty years, he felt the sharp sting of inadequacy.[①]

---

① Shao Li: *My Quality of Life*, People's Literature Publishing House, 2004, p. 35.

At university, Wang Qilong's inability to speak Mandarin and his thick Western Henan accent made him a target of ridicule, reducing him to a withdrawn and silent figure. He dared not pursue romance, remaining isolated throughout his college years. Despite his academic excellence, upon graduation he was assigned to a provincial backwater due to his rural origins. Years later, though Wang Qilong had climbed the social ladder to become an official in Yangcheng—outwardly possessing all the trappings of success—the indelible marks of his upbringing remained. "That slight protrusion of bone on the inner ankle," a physical manifestation of his peasant roots, became a source of shame when confronted with the delicate, smooth feet of Annie, his urban-bred love interest, laying bare his enduring inferiority complex. Wang Qilong, a youth from the countryside, had been wrestling with his identity his entire life. For him, "becoming an urbanite, becoming an official, he had gained new identities and new consciousness, yet his original identity continued to haunt him, leaving him lost in the chaos and fragmentation of multiple identities and conflicting consciousnesses." "Wang Qilong hated his village-born wife, yet only with her could he truly be a man. When facing urban women—those untouched by earth or the smell of kitchen smoke—he found himself impotent. Thus, 'my quality of life' was inevitably low."①

What is particularly commendable is how the author consistently explores the deeper implications of the urban-rural divide—the psychological

① Liu Xianqin and Shao Li: "Quality of Life Depends on Self-Perception: An Interview with Writer Shao Li", China Reading Weekly, July 13, 2005.

oppression wrought by material disparities. For Wang Qilong, despite being an outstanding young man from the countryside, the indelible stamp of his rural origins perpetuates feelings of inferiority and timidity. Though the story ultimately reduces humanity's conquest of the city to Wang Qilong's ambiguous domination over Annie—a Beijing native who symbolizes urbanity—thereby somewhat diminishing the work's social scope, its final line remains profoundly moving:"Though we are all people striving to live, our lives remain so utterly unmoored." This heavy conclusion lays bare the rootlessness of modern existence.

The novella *Minghui's Christmas* tells the story of a woman's downward spiral in the city. Minghui was once the village prodigy—"after three years of junior high in the township and three more of senior high in the county, she carried herself with the regal poise of a princess in her village." The unexpected failure in her college entrance exams became the first crisis in her privileged life.

Unable to endure the villagers' veiled barbs and venomous gossip—especially after witnessing the dazzling urban transformation of her former neighbor, Taozi—Minghui too chose to leave for the city. Minghui's objectives were ruthlessly clear: to earn money, buy urban property, and establish permanent residency—"I'll have my babies in the city! I'll make them urbanites—I, Yuanyuan, will be a city mother!" This pursuit of quick wealth and metropolitan identity began with her transformation from Minghui to

"Yuanyuan," adopting this pseudonym while working at a massage parlor, where prostitution became her fastest path to financial accumulation.

In this process, Minghui met Li Yangqun, a divorced urban youth who became her client and was a man of admirable qualities. The two shared a certain spiritual compatibility. Later, Minghui moved into Li Yangqun's home, finally attaining the urban life she had always dreamed of.

"It was on that year's Christmas Eve that Yuan Yuan (Minghui) began living in Li Yangqun's house."

Yuan Yuan kept Li Yangqun's home in perfect order.

Day after day, Yuan Yuan grew increasingly idle at home. With workers handling every chore—even feeding the goldfish or watering the plants became tasks beneath her effort—she spent her days sleeping, watching television. Occasionally, she would stroll through the shops alone or indulge in saunas and beauty treatments. The woman who once served others now found herself being served. The attendants rushed to fawn over her, eagerly helping her remove the coat, exclaiming how her complexion had grown fairer, how beautiful she looked, how exquisite her clothes and jewelry were. In barely over a year, her world had transformed beyond recognition. Yuan Yuan was now dressed in increasingly expensive outfits. Her full, moon-shaped face—framed by plump earlobes that hung thick with good fortune—drew admiration from every woman who saw her. "What a blessed destiny," they would murmur.

Perhaps this was precisely the life Yuan Yuan had always dreamed of—yet now that she lived it, her heart felt as hollow as an abandoned warehouse.

The following Christmas, Minghui eagerly went out with Li Yangqun to celebrate. Yet when she encountered his companions, she realized Li blended seamlessly among them—"like a sheep returning to its flock, his demeanor perfectly attuned to their rhythms." These women wore avant-garde jewelry, their pinkies arched delicately as they held glasses. They smoked openly among men, exuding elegance—while Yuan Yuan's old friends had puffed furtively in back rooms, their smoking slovenly and illicit. Yuan Yuan relaxed slightly, relieved by their inattention. The smoke they exhaled coiled like a river, yet she felt stranded on the opposite bank. They drank freely; she sipped her lemon-infused Corona. The women exuded superiority, audacity, and nobility. They came in all shapes—some plump, some slender; some tall, some short; their complexions ranging from fair to dark. Yet without exception, they brimmed with a confidence that rendered them both radiant and imperious. They laughed and bantered with uninhibited joy—this was their city, after all. It struck her then: the city would always belong to urbanites. "How could Yuan Yuan ever move in their circles? She was just Yuan Yuan—never could she become one of them!" Facing the irreversible truth of her unbelonging, this desolation propelled Yuan Yuan toward suicide. And Li Yangqun—perplexed to the end—could only wonder: Why would she do such a thing?

From Wang Qilong to Minghui, Shao Li's deeper concern lies in a fundamental question: How can the human spirit find anchorage in the city? While urban life offers avenues for material accumulation through striving and ambition, the existential drift—that profound sense of rootlessness and spiritual homelessness—remains unresolved. This crisis of belonging cuts deeper than any material lack. The concept of the "Stranger" (also translated as the Outsider or the Foreigner) was first proposed by Georg Simmel, who defined this figure as "not the wanderer who comes today and leaves tomorrow, but rather the one who arrives today and stays tomorrow—the potential wanderer who, though remaining, has not wholly forgotten the freedom to come and go." These strangers drift through the city, their fates suspended in anonymity. Who, then, bears witness to their lives? This becomes the author's relentless inquiry.

Not coincidentally, Qiao Ye's debut novel *I Truly Love You* (originally titled *Tight-Lipped* when serialized in *Chinese Writers*, No. 10, 2003; published as a standalone volume by Changjiang Literature & Art Press in 2004) traces the tragic trajectory of twin sisters whose plunge into urban life ends in moral disintegration under the corrosive force of money. The elder sister initially came to the city out of poverty, seeking work to fund her younger sister's education. Yet urban life gradually reshaped her, reducing her to a commodified existence. Eventually, she even attempted to school her sister in the power of money:

"With money, you can do almost anything."

With money, I'd never again have to toil under the sun, bent over barren soil. Never again scrape a living from dirt clods for mere survival. Never again endure the likes of Yang Shouquan's contempt.

With money, I could buy an apartment in the most exclusive compound, open a boutique fruit shop or florist on the busiest avenue, and become a leisurely businesswoman. In short, only with money can we truly be kind to ourselves.

Guided by this warped value system, the younger sister quickly succumbed, joining her sibling in prostitution to chase the elder's million-yuan dream. Qiao Ye later revealed this narrative drew from transformations in her hometown, where young women left to work, earned fast money, and rapidly upgraded their families' material conditions. It could be said that when the tidal wave of that era struck, it scoured away moral boundaries entirely. This explains why Leng Hong in *I Truly Love You* even sabotages her sister's romance—binding her to their shared pursuit of profit. Seduced by money, "they incrementally surrendered their dignity to compromise." Though Qiao Ye's debut novel demonstrates a profound inquiry into human nature and a passionate engagement with life, it nonetheless portrays the city as a gravitational abyss of desire. What stands out is the author's relentless probing of a pivotal question: If initial moral compromises were forced by circumstance, why does self-indulgence persist? Is there some inertial pull—or perhaps a warping of humanity itself? This remains the text's most trenchant provocation.

Even at this juncture, the author still affirms the redemptive power of human connection. She constructs Zhang Zhaohui as Love's ultimatum—a boyfriend who, fully aware of Leng Zi's fall, still reaches across the moral chasm to salvage her. His appearance briefly rekindled in Leng Zi a sense of life's warmth and happiness. She left the bathhouse behind and took up temporary work at Zhang Zhaohui's hospital, embarking on what seemed like a new beginning. Yet fate took another turn: Leng Zi died while trying to save her sister. In her final letter, she posed the question—"Do you believe in hell, or in heaven?"—a challenge that ultimately pierced her sister's hardened heart, propelling her toward genuine renewal.

It becomes evident that both women writers focus their lens on the destinies of urban newcomers—their struggles, their falls, and their inner psychological journeys. As Lavelle insightfully noted, "Art is the expression of society; when it soars to its highest realm, it articulates the most progressive social currents—it becomes both pioneer and prophet." Thus, to determine whether art has truly fulfilled its function as a harbinger, or whether an artist genuinely belongs to the avant-garde, we must first discern where humanity is headed—we must understand the very trajectory of our collective destiny."[①] In tracing these urban migrants' psychological odysseys, literature emerges as society's scribe, meticulously documenting the complexities of lived experience and the kaleidoscope of human existence.

3. The Multitudes Within *Weakness*

Zhang Yu's novel *Weakness* (People's Literature Publishing House, 2000) stands as a profound crystallization of the author's urban meditations and metropolitan consciousness. Having established his literary reputation in the 1980s with works like *Living Ghost*—penetrating critiques of historical trauma—Zhang Yu, in *Weakness*, channels his vision through the lives of two ordinary policemen, using their stories to dissect the interplay between urbanity and human nature. The text employs Chunhua's contemplation of roads as a revelatory lens to expose the divide between urban and rural existence.

In the countryside, Chunhua never lost her way. But in the city, she could never seem to remember the roads. No matter how many paths crisscrossed the rural landscape—each one distinct, shaped by the unique slopes it traversed, the particular riverbanks it followed, the specific crop fields it bordered, even the individual trees that lined it—not a single road repeated

① (US) Matei Călinescu: *Five Faces of Modernity: Modernism, Avant-Garde, Decadence, Kitsch, Postmodernism*, translated by Gu Aibin and Li Ruihua, Yilin Press, 2015, p. 114.

itself. A single journey was all it took to etch them permanently in her mind. The city's roads were different—so many of them identical, flanked by indistinguishable buildings, uniform intersections, even cookie-cutter trees lining the sidewalks. To navigate, you had to memorize cold statistics: the third intersection, then left at the fifth... One misremembered digit, and you were lost. Eventually, Chunhua realized: rural wayfinding relied on sensory memory, while urban navigation demanded logical calculation...①

Chunhua's labyrinthine struggle with roads mirrors the author's own. In The Birth of a Withered Tree, Zhang Yu confesses: "I've never understood why urban streets terrify me. The sight of intersections triggers panic—disorientation so profound I can't discern cardinal directions. I lack the sun-reading instinct rural living teaches. Some skills, I've learned, defy academic acquisition. My home was in the mountains—there, I navigated by ridges and gullies, by waterways and trees, by stones. My mind grasped roads through sensory memory. But in the city, where buildings and intersections blur into sameness, my memory finds no purchase. Urbanites memorize through logic; such thinking will never be mine."② This fundamental urban-rural dichotomy left authors struggling to adapt—their early life memories and behavioral patterns were so deeply ingrained that even decades after settling in cities and achieving success, many post-1950s generation writers still defiantly

---

① Zhang Yu: *Weakness*, People's Literature Publishing House, 2000, p. 73.

② Zhang Yu: "The Birth of a Withered Tree", in Urban Wanderings: Selected Short and Medium-Length Fiction by Zhang Yu, Huaxia Publishing House, 1997, p. 478.

declared: "I am a farmer!" Take Jia Pingwa, for instance—his unapologetic adherence to farmer ways: slurping noodles with gusto, squatting to eat his meals. Or Yan Lianke in *My Ancestors*, where kinship ties run as thick and vital as the veins of the earth itself. And Mo Yan, who declares in *I Will Always Know Where I Came From*—mapping his life's journey back to the very soil that shaped him. These practices represent their steadfast commitment to self-awareness and literary authenticity. Yet how do such writers articulate their urban consciousness? Perhaps their works themselves hold the answer.

In the postscript to *Weakness*, the author reveals that the novel emerged from over a decade of living in Zhengzhou, by which point he no longer felt like an outsider, his moral consciousness gradually sharpening. This fictional narrative became his medium for processing complex urban attachments. Indeed, this is a work that channels the author's urban experiences and articulates an emerging metropolitan consciousness. By centering two ordinary police officers—anti-pickpocketing squad members who daily grapple with thieves—the narrative positions them as frontline guardians of the city's fragile order. Yu Fugui is a seasoned officer whose exceptional skills earn the police chief's favor, yet he faces relentless ostracization within his squad. At home, his impotence persists—his meager salary fails to sustain the family, forcing his laid-off wife to peddle fabric from a tricycle to make ends meet. The other protagonist, Wang Hai, is a capable young man whose college-era political involvement left him with a permanent stain—barred from Party membership and career advancement, he partners with Yu Fugui. Both men embody stoic contentment in poverty, diligent yet burdened by unspoken frustrations. As model citizens, they too must live and survive, supporting families while confronting—like all urban dwellers—the relentless grind and seduction of money. However noble their calling, however radiant their virtue, they gradually awaken to the crude truth: "What matters most? Money matters most." "The market economy darts ahead like a hare, with humanity chasing like panting hounds—or perhaps it's the very sky itself, leaving us as kites with severed strings, adrift in its vast indifference."①

The twin narratives of these policemen intertwine with stark social realities: the tragic descent of a shampoo girl into vice, hoodlums monopolizing market stalls, a police chief torn between official duty and personal conscience, and even thieves upholding their own code of honor—complete with clandestine congresses. Even Yu Fugui—the seemingly most upright man in others' eyes—harbors a buried transgression: he once succumbed to temptation and slept with his sister-in-law. His moral quagmire lays bare the existential and psychological struggles of urban society's ordinary people. The author deliberately constructs Wang Hai as an ideological counterpoint—a man who rejects his first girlfriend's offer to relocate to Shanghai for marriage, steadfast in his professional convictions. Yet when faced with his second romance, a wealthy heiress, he struggles to navigate the class divide.

---

① Zhang Yu: *Weakness,* People's Literature Publishing House, 2000, p. 161.

Even this paragon of principle feels the sting when his father sells years-worth of root carvings to fund his wedding. In such nuanced moments, the novel achieves rare emotional veracity. Wang Hai's parents were ordinary factory workers. His father, a devoted bonsai enthusiast, deliberately chose a cramped ground-floor apartment during housing allocation to nurture his potted landscapes. Though deeply knowledgeable and emotionally invested in this art, he ultimately sold his prized specimens to fund his son's marriage. In these unassuming details, the novel renders working-class lives with tender precision—and subtly encodes the author's own urban critique and idealism.

4. The Cyclical Nature of The Book of Life

Li Peifu's *The Book of Life* (Writer's Publishing House, 2012) opens with a striking declaration: "I am a seed. I have transplanted myself into the city." And later: "At times, I feel like a wedge—a willow wedge forcibly driven into the cracks of the urban landscape." He confessed: "I spent fifty years preparing for this manuscript, and five to six years writing it. Over these years, drafts were written, discarded, and rewritten—when utterly stuck, I'd return to my hometown to rediscover inspiration. The opening alone took over a year to perfect. I had to find that inaugural sentence—it would dictate my linguistic bearing, my narrative tone... Whether the writing flowed or faltered, there was always this sensation of 'fingernails blooming.'"①

The story begins with the author inhaling the city's essence—its odors both literal and metaphysical.

This is a city nestled against the Yellow River, its historical memory steeped in that gritty, sandy scent. Over time, the river's sediments have been ground to dust—fine as flour, yet still unmistakably sand: a mingling of grit, astringency, the fishy tang of water, and faint notes of sweetness and salt. It is also a crossroads—a nation's crossroads. Railways and flight routes stitch together its east-west, north-south axes. And long before, it was the Yellow and Huai Rivers that wove the city's watery thoroughfares... a place where all paths converge. Now you understand—this plains-city is fundamentally a crossroads of perpetual comings and goings. Though merely a "crossroads," its historical sediment runs unfathomably deep. So let us focus on this junction alone: here surge tides of migrants from all directions. It is a place that erases memory as readily as it fetishizes novelty—its commercial ethos etched in the marrow, both hostile to outsiders and paranoid of them, thriving on one-off transactions with no need for repeat customers. Yet linger long enough, and it reveals an unexpected temperament: tolerant, conservative,

---

① Zhang Yali: "The Book of Life: The Story of Central Plains is the Story of China", China Youth Daily, October 23, 2015.

even loyal.[①]

This work is regarded as the culminating chapter of Li Peifu's "Plains Trilogy." Since the 1990s with *The Gate of Sheep*, Li has meticulously excavated the ethos and psyche of the plains—that sheep-headed sliver of land in central Henan, a microscopic yet potent fragment of China's 9.6 million square kilometers. "How did they survive—those generations weathering endless wars and relentless disasters? How did their descendants persist? No one truly knows. Yet in the blink of an eye, three millennia have passed. Across the vast Central Henan Plains, villages still cluster, chimney smoke still rises... People endure, trees endure. Three thousand years—and all that remains is this whispered legacy: a land deemed 'sheep-soil.'"[②] The author created this land's sovereign—Hu Tiancheng—who cultivates trees and people with equal mastery, commanding wind and rain, embodying the pinnacle of Central Plains' power dynamics. Post-2000 works like The City's Lights chronicle rural migrants' ruthless urban odysseys during China's reform era. By contrast, The Book of Life unfolds with vaster complexity: its very first sentence plants a seed forcibly grafted onto urban soil. Critics have hailed the work as "grander in scope, more expansive, and pulsating with primal vitality. In my post-Mao Dun Literary Award interview, I encapsulated *The Book of Life* thus: "It interrogates the earth while bearing witness to mortal toils—the

---

① Li Peifu: *The Book of Life*, Writer's Publishing House, 2012, p. 7.

② Li Peifu: *The Gate of Sheep*, Huaxia Publishing House, 1999, p. 4.

definitive synthesis of China's urban-rural narrative."

From the hunger-stricken years of his childhood to his current stature as a celebrated writer, Li Peifu's journey spans over five decades—a path he and his generation traversed with extraordinary resilience. Through life and literature, his understanding of this land and its people has undergone a profound metamorphosis. In the 1980s, Li Peifu decried money as the root of all evil—a conviction crystallized in his novel The Golden House, where a gleaming mansion shatters an ancient village's tranquility, unleashing torrents of desire. By the 21st century, he reversed his verdict: poverty, especially spiritual poverty, became the true malignancy. "The damage wrought by poverty," he concluded, "eclipses corruption by wealth."① The 9th Mao Dun Literary Award's citation for *The Book of Life* proclaimed: "This novel's essence lies in its exploration of epoch and humanity. Amid the seismic shift from rural traditions to urban modernity, Li Peifu illuminates those who 'carry the land upon their backs.'" With the ambition of classical realism, he believes character and destiny can reveal the deep structures of social consciousness. *The Book of Life* crafts vivid characters through masterful prose—individuals caught between speed and slowness, gain and loss, homeland and exile, matter and spirit. Their souls, tested through relentless turbulence, embody the transitional contradictions that mirror society's own metamorphosis with urgent precision. Li Peifu's *The Book of Life* is like the vast

---

① Jin Tao: "Illuminating Life Through Insight: Henan Writers' Association Chair Li Peifu on His New Work <The Book of Life>", China Art News, April 9, 2012.

plains he so deeply loves - on this broad and profound land, it faithfully preserves the footprints of the times. The urban landscapes depicted in *The Book of Life* more resemble a black hole of desires: insatiable cravings of fellow villagers, the madness and inflation of camel traders chasing gold, and Abyssinian roses shipped from three continents representing beautiful ideals. These objects of desire—once obsessively pursued—proved powerless to fill the void within. Thus, the author brings his protagonist full circle, back to his roots. "For my back has grown countless 'eyes'—yet I cannot tell whether this parched, wandering leaf can ever return to its branch?"

In *The Book of Life*, the story starts with a resolute tale of leaving. As a seed forcibly grafted into the city, Wu Zhipeng attends university, pursues graduate studies, gains employment and settles down—yet unable to endure constant disturbances from hometown relatives and unbearable burdens exceeding his means, he finally chooses escape, extricating himself from that oppressive shadow. After realizing his life ambitions, earning enough money, and achieving sufficient success, he found he must go back. In the hospital, only during those four hours each night when sleeping on two sedatives could he forget himself. All other time was spent retracing the past—"like movie film replaying over and over"—"if only time could flow backward." Wu Zhipeng brought the pomegranate plant back to the village, only to realize: "For me, I originally believed hometown was just a dialect, a voice, an attitude—something you can't avoid or discard, a kind of entanglement, or rather a heavy burden carried on one's back. But as I traveled further away, as years began growing mold, I finally understood—that endless yellow earth was the only thing capable of holding me down."① His "return" serves as a metaphor for the urban migrant's spiritual dilemma—how to find solace while adrift in the relentless pursuit of wealth and desire, and ultimately, how to reconcile with one's fractured psyche.

It is undeniable that with social progress and the dissolution of grand narratives, writers have increasingly focused on individual destinies. Compared to rural settings, urban units offer relative freedom and simplicity—their narratives are inherently individualistic and private, unburdened by the entrenched constraints of familial traditions and communal legacies. This shift explains the evolution in Li Peifu's works: from the power discourses of *The Gate of Sheep* to the personal narratives of *The Book of Life*. The French New Novelist Alain Robbe-Grillet once observed: "Every society and era favors a novelistic form that implicitly affirms an order—a particular mode of thought and being in the world."② In the 1990s, literature broke free from political constraints, and its compass shifted toward market forces. Cities became the premier stage for expressing reality under market principles. No longer mere backdrops to literary narratives—passively serving charac-

① Li Peifu: *The Book of Life*, Writer's Publishing House, 2012, p. 424.

② Lai Daren (ed.): 1990s Literary Criticism Series: Aesthetic Romanticism and Moral Idealism, Huaxia Publishing House, 2000, p. 10.

ters—urban spaces emerged as autonomous entities that both powerfully allure and oppress. "Each social group offers its own way of reading the city."[①] Therefore, we can observe different authors' portrayals of cities and their literary expressions—the varied ways they provide for understanding urban spaces, as well as the living conditions and survival states of urban dwellers within modern contexts.

① (US) Richard Lehan: *The City in Literature: An Intellectual and Cultural History*, translated by Wu Zifeng, Shanghai People's Publishing House, 2009, p. 11.

Chapter 5

Bygone Relics: Memory and Identity in the Interstices of History and Reality

The American philosopher, essayist, and poet Ralph Waldo Emerson once asserted: "Cities exist by virtue of memory." What defines a city's identity? New York's quintessential cultural symbols—the Statue of Liberty, the Metropolitan Museum, Wall Street, Broadway; London's British Museum and Big Ben; Paris' Louvre, Eiffel Tower, and Champs-Élysées—all serve as iconic urban markers. Similarly, "urban symbols refer to iconic elements that epitomize a city's cultural identity—carriers of heritage value, leaving indelible impressions and civic pride. These encompass historical relics, flora, notable figures, landmarks, and significant architecture. They serve as the city's 'calling card,' embodying its spirit and cultural legacy."① For urban literature, city symbols serve as vital vessels—preserving historical memory, signifying civic spirit, and bearing urban consciousness. This holds equally true for Henan, where bygone urban relics—architecture, folk customs, and local landmarks—carry forward the continuum of collective memory.

1. Kaifeng's Old Streets and Alleys

Daniel Bell once remarked that a city is not merely a place, but a state of mind—a symbol of a distinctive lifestyle characterized by diversity and vibrancy... To truly know a city, one must walk its streets. In the literary realm, the avenues of Paris have acquired historical and cultural resonance through the writings of Hugo, Zola, Baudelaire, and Benjamin.

① Liu Yihai: "*On Urban Symbols*", Urban Development Studies, No. 1, 2008.

Kaifeng's ancient streets and alleys stand as testaments to the city's glorious past.

I hold an unwavering criterion for judging cities: their streets should never weary the wanderer. Only two meet this standard—Beijing, with its labyrinthine hutongs around Houhai and Qianmen, and Kaifeng, where a tapestry of alleys unfolds within the embrace of ancient city walls.

Xianren Alley, Nanjiaojing Hutong, Caoshi Street, Lishiting Street, Leguan Street, Caomen South Street, Weizhong Front and Back Streets, Roast Chicken Hutong, Qingping North-South Streets, Iron Goddess Temple Street, Nanyangshi Street, Front Chaomi Hutong, Rear Chaomi Hutong, Peichanggong Hutong, East Banjie Street, Youfang Hutong, Yajue Hutong, Dayuankeng Riverside Street, Wushengjiao Street, Daxian Hutong, Bogeshi Street, Cunde Lane...

Even the names alone—let alone the streets themselves—hint at buried narratives. Take Qidao Street: its etymology traces to the Banner and Pennant Temple (Qidao Miao). What did this temple look like? The street even splits into Greater Qidao and Lesser Qidao along Daliang Road's axis. Yanzhi River Street (Rouge River Street) housed residents along its banks. As many were Hui Muslims slaughtering sheep and cattle, blood flowed into the river, turning it red—thus the elegant name "Rouge River." Another theory suggests brothel women in adjacent towers washed their makeup into the river, giving it a rouge hue, hence the name. Then there's Bogeshi Street (Pigeon

Market Street). Boge? Dictionary research reveals it refers to a specific pigeon breed—gray-black plumage with crimson necks and chests, also called domestic pigeons. Did the street earn its name from this avian trade? As for Chaomi Hutong (Fried Rice Alley), its very name seems to waft the aroma of toasted grains and hearth smoke. There are also Shaoji Hutong (Roast Chicken Hutong), Cuihua Hutong (Jade Flower Hutong), Machixian Hutong (Purslane Hutong), Heimo Hutong (Black Ink Hutong), Daxian Hutong (Thread-Spinning Hutong), Shuiche Hutong (Waterwheel Hutong), Xuanjiang Hutong (Lathe-Craftsman Hutong), Chunshu Hutong (Toon Tree Hutong), Xiuqiu Hutong (Hydrangea Hutong), Nianzi Street (Imperial Carriage Street), Tushi Street (Earthen Market Street), Caoshi Street (Hay Market Street), Yuchi Yan Street (Fishpond Riverside Street), Sanyanjing Street (Three-Well Street), Madao Street (Horse Path Street)... These names evoke nostalgia and a yearning for nature, while conjuring images of Kaifeng's bustling folk arts and diverse petty commodities.

These streets and alleys, imbued with rustic charm, form vital threads in Kaifeng's historical tapestry. Yet as time marches on, many have vanished—demolished in the city's relentless urban renewal campaigns. Historical records indicate that Kaifeng had 58 hutongs in 1898 (24th year of Qing Guangxu reign). By the Republican era (1912-1949), this number grew to 78. Post-1949 urban renewal gradually reduced the count to 62 in 1983, though a temporary rebound to 75 occurred by 1990. The most dramatic decline came in the 1990s—plummeting to 52 by 1999, marking a loss of 23 hutongs in just nine years. For instance, the once-famous Xiuqiu Hutong (Hydrangea Hutong) near Stone Bridge Crossing, along with the former residence of Su Xiaomei within it, has completely vanished. Likewise, Erduoyan Hutong (Earhole Hutong), north of the Municipal Children's Hospital, was entirely demolished during redevelopment. Jiangcu Hutong (Soy Vinegar Hutong) disappeared during the renovation of Shudian Street (Bookstore Street) and Shanhuodian Street (Grocery Market Street). Meanwhile, Changshou Street (Longevity Street)—originally located southwest of the Wuchao Gate (Meridian Gate) Plaza—derived its name from an archway at its eastern end bearing the inscription "Boundless Longevity," which once stood before the Meridian Gate itself. These alleys, each carrying fragments of Kaifeng's living history, have now been erased from the urban fabric. To this day, many urban landmarks have vanished amid old-city redevelopment, with historical traces utterly erased. Yet certain books documenting urban memory have preserved these historical landscapes with remarkable fidelity.

Mr. Guan Aihe's *Kaifeng Memory* cites a 2005 *New York Times* article titled "*From Kaifeng to New York—Glory Is as Ephemeral as Smoke and Clouds*," written by the renowned columnist Nicholas Kristof. Regarding Kaifeng, the author writes:

Today's Kaifeng is dirty and poor, no longer even a provincial capital—its status is insignificant, lacking even an airport. This decline lays bare the impermanence of wealth and prosperity. In the 11th century, however, Kaifeng served as the capital of the Song Dynasty, with a population exceeding one million, while London at the time had merely around 15,000 inhabitants.

The Qingming Shanghe Tu (*Along the River During the Qingming Festival*), now housed in the Palace Museum in Beijing, measures 24.8 cm in height and 528.7 cm in length. It vividly depicts the bustling urban scenery and natural landscapes of Bianliang (modern-day Kaifeng), the capital of the Northern Song Dynasty, during the Qingming Festival. Street vendors hawk their wares along crowded thoroughfares, while throngs of people jostle shoulder-to-shoulder. Camel caravans from the Western Regions, traversing the ancient Silk Road, arrive laden with goods, soliciting trade in the marketplace. Teahouses, inns, and wine shops stand in tight rows, their thriving businesses evident at a glance. The stark contrast between historical splendor and present decline has become a recurring motif in literary works, with many writers tracing the fading afterglow of Kaifeng's past. As an ancient capital, the city once radiated cultural brilliance, yet now occupies a position of relative underdevelopment. Recent waves of urban renewal have further eroded its architectural heritage, as soaring high-rises, modernist landmarks, and relentless development priorities increasingly obscure the city's distinctive character. Through literary documentation, however, we rediscover this historic city's singular charm.

2. *Lao Zabanr*: Recollections of Zhengzhou

Lao Zabanr (*Old Assorted Memories*) is a collection of short stories by Chen Tiejun, published by Henan Literature and Art Publishing House in 1999. The author's family has lived in Zhengzhou for generations, and the work draws from stories told by his grandfather, who once served as director of the Hewuju (River Conservancy Bureau). The narrative begins: "Outside Zhengzhou's West Gate lay a place called Laofengang (Old Burial Mound)—originally a wilderness of ancient graves where spirits whispered, until the successive openings of the Longhai and Pinghan Railways transformed Zhengzhou from a dust-choked town into a thriving commercial hub." *Lao Zabanr* assembles Zhengzhou's folk memories, blending street life, extraordinary tales, and local customs into a rare literary portrait of old Zhengzhou.

The work first depicts the sanjiu liuliu (literally "three teachings and nine schools")—the diverse social strata and street life of Zhengzhou's Laofengang. The opening story introduces Chen Dapao, a marketplace storyteller whose uniqueness lay in his subversion of convention: "Rejecting traditional tales of emperors, generals, and beauties—with their moralizing lectures on loyalty, filial piety, and virtue—he instead drew material from real-life events around him. Improvising satirical skits filled with innuendo and allegory, he directed caustic ridicule at societal ills: feudal ethics, vulgar customs, warlord elites, corrupt officials, petty opportunists, and street ruffians all became targets of his scathing performances." It was precisely this unconventional and groundbreaking approach that set him apart from the myriad jianghu (outlaw/martial arts world) figures at Laofengang. He bore no resemblance to those peddling cheap remedies for a living, but rather evoked the spirit of folk literati like Feng Menglong and Pu Songling.[①]

Yet such an unyielding and contrarian folk artist inevitably paid the price for his temperament. "First, the Laofengang *bao* chief tried to expel him from the area without explanation, citing 'moral corruption.' Then, the local underworld—humiliated by his verbal attacks—seized him like 'an eagle snatching a chick' and beat him severely. Subsequently, police bureaus under the warlords Wu and Feng detained him for months without trial. Finally, the Japanese military police subjected him repeatedly to torture—countless sessions on the '*tiger bench*' with chili water forced down his throat."[②] Even after the founding of New China, when the new government assigned him work as a state-salaried performer in a *quyi* (folk art) troupe, misfortune still pursued him. During the 1957 zhengfeng (rectification) campaign, he was branded a Rightist for alleged "anti-Party remarks," beginning his long ordeal in provincial labor reform teams. Only after the fall of the *Gang of Four* did he safely return to Zhengzhou, where he eventually ended his tormented life

---

① Chen Tiejun. Lao *Zabanr* (*Old Assorted Memories*). Zhengzhou: Henan Literature and Art Publishing House, 1999, p. 2.

② Chen Tiejun. Lao *Zabanr* (*Old Assorted Memories*). Zhengzhou: Henan Literature and Art Publishing House, 1999, p. 5-6.

amid continued vilification. The narrative thus interweaves vivid characterization with socio-historical forces.

Secondly, the work documents Zhengzhou's urban transformations upon entering the industrial-commercial era. The *Grudge* recounts the city's first foreign resident—an American missionary the locals called "Big-Nosed Shi"—who crossed oceans and traversed mountains to reach Zhengzhou. He rented two civilian houses on Yamenqian Street (Street Before the Magistrate's Office) to proselytize Christian doctrine. Thus did Zhengzhou gain its first bona fide foreign resident. With his assistance, the city's first missionary hospital—Huamei Hospital (Sino-American Hospital)—was established. "At its peak, the hospital employed dozens of foreign medical staff. Their selfless dedication and advanced medical techniques quickly earned public trust, enabling the mission's influence to expand rapidly throughout Zhengzhou." Later, with the completion of the Longhai and Pinghan Railways, Zhengzhou evolved into a pivotal transportation hub connecting north and south—a nodal point for goods distribution. Waves of foreign entrepreneurs arrived, establishing banks, trading firms, textile mills, amusement halls, and Western restaurants, until foreign faces became ubiquitous across the city. With the Japanese invasion, Zhengzhou temporarily became a sphere of foreign dominance.

It was against this backdrop of international convergence that psychological undercurrents emerged—a covert clash of attitudes, as locals grew increasingly hostile toward foreigners. Gradually, people ceased referring to them by nationality, instead collectively branding them yang guizi ("foreign devils"). Mr. Shao, a prominent Zhengzhou merchant, orchestrated a remarkable act of symbolic defiance. He deliberately selected Fred—a struggling foreign resident—and paid him handsomely to pull Mr. Shao in a rickshaw through Zhengzhou's streets for an entire day. The spectacle achieved instant notoriety. This carefully staged inversion of the colonial power dynamic elated local onlookers—cheering crowds reveled in what they saw as restored national dignity and the humiliation of foreign arrogance. Yet the foreigner, now a China hand, took the money and swiftly transformed from beggar to patron in the brothels, privately scoffing at the Zhengzhou locals as fools. This historical retrieval enriches Zhengzhou's urban memory. Conventional narratives portray Republican-era Zhengzhou as neither a provincial capital nor an industrial hub—merely an impoverished town ravaged by famine and war. Chen Tiejun's account, however, reveals a city undergoing parallel modernization: emerging industries, foreign influences, and undocumented urban cultures that had been suppressed within dominant historical discourses.

Thirdly, the work vividly captures Zhengzhou's local vernacular, eccentric characters, and fading urban traces—each element a palimpsest of the city's living history.

"Ye Xian'er" (The Unorthodox Mystic) stands as a distinctive literary piece. The term "Ye Xian'er", originating from Zhengzhou dialect, "typically refers to two types of individuals: folk healers and itinerant charlatans. Here, it specifically denotes those among them who lack legitimate origins and engage in wildly unconventional practices. In other words, those branded as Ye Xian'er were invariably unscrupulous practitioners of heterodox arts."① The story's Ye Xian'er—a certain Mr. Hu—operated his dubious trade on South Main Street.

At that time, South Main Street was renowned as an herbal medicine emporium, with over a hundred pharmacies lining the street—not only local vendors but even Yuzhou merchants with centuries-old traditions maintained stalls there. In those days, most 'mystics' operated pharmacies while practicing medicine; the density of drugstores attested to the abundance of skilled healers. The most renowned was "Wanshenggong" Herbal Pharmacy by Xiong'er River's Deji Bridge, its entrance flanked by couplets:

Left scroll: "This is the Art of Benevolence"

Right scroll: "How Dare We Claim Mere Minor Remedies?"

Horizontal plaque: "Delivering the World and Reviving Lives"

---

① Chen Tiejun. Lao *Zabanr* (*Old Assorted Memories*). Zhengzhou: Henan Literature and Art Publishing House, 1999, p. 157.

The grandeur of these proclamations spoke volumes. The proprietor, Master Gao Xian'er, came from generations of healers—educated in Confucian classics before apprenticing in his father's practice. Whether he truly "revived lives" remains debatable, but his commitment to benevolent healing was undeniable. For impoverished families, he often dispensed medicine freely, and for those unable to settle their debts, he wrote off their accounts without hesitation. During epidemics, he would pour sack upon sack of herbs into public wells, ensuring water-drawing households had preventive remedies. His reputation for compassion spread far, attracting endless streams of patients seeking his care. This Hu Xian'er, however, stood notably apart. He was South Main Street's sole practitioner who healed without selling medicine—because his methods required none. Instead, he relied entirely on unorthodox and startling folk techniques.①

The text then recounts Hu Xian'er's unorthodox medical practices through startling anecdotes: he would treat children's dormant pox rashes by deliberately exposing them to mosquito bites, believing the resulting irritation and desperate cries would force the rashes to surface; similarly, he addressed difficult childbirths by pricking the mother's abdomen with an ordinary sewing needle, which reportedly enabled smooth deliveries through this abrupt intervention. Hu Xian'er's growing renown on South Main Street ultimately brought calamity—after treating a Japanese officer's leg wound, he

① Ibid., pp. 157-158.

fell victim to retaliatory Nationalist forces and vanished without explanation. Whether executed as a hanjian (collaborator) or forcibly conscripted as a military medic remains a matter of speculative whispers. This tale encapsulates both the skilled compassion of traditional healers and the supernatural mystique of jianghu charlatans (Ye Xian'er), offering a poignant distillation of the eccentric characters and extraordinary events that flourished during the Republic's chaotic years.

This collection of stories excavates folk memory in its raw vitality—whether through "*Divine Judgment*," "*The Colossal Bandit*," "*The Goat-Beggar*," "*The Bodyguard*," "*The Sedan Carrier*," "*The Commoner*," or "*The Lame Man*." Each narrative channels the inexhaustible resilience of grassroots life, simultaneously serving as an archaeological hook into that historical moment. The work intertwines the historical legacy of Cai's Restaurant on Dehua Street with the multifaceted lives of sedan carriers, while its vivid depictions of alleyway cultures, wedding/funeral customs, tales of city gods and rogue mystics, and authentic Zhengzhou dialect collectively render it a panoramic novel of urban folkways. Through meticulous narration, it resurrects long-buried historical details of old Zhengzhou.

3. Visual-Textual Memory and Cultural Imagination

Since the 1990s, against the backdrop of a cultural nostalgia boom, the popular Old City Series books have extensively documented urban landmarks across China, excavating their historical connotations and cultural significance. These include the Qinhuai River in Nanjing, Guangzhou's arcade buildings, Xi'an's Forest of Steles and Giant Wild Goose Pagoda, and Wuhan's Yellow Crane Tower—each serving as sedimentations of urban history, culture, and values, becoming psychological-cultural symbols deeply embedded in civic identity.

Edited by Meng Xianming, *Pictorial Old Zhengzhou* (2004, Zhongzhou Ancient Books Publishing House) anchors its narrative in the city's *3,600-year capital history*—having served successively as prefecture, administrative district, and county seat, all within present-day Guancheng District. The Erqi Memorial Tower, now the city center, stands where literati giants Su Dongpo and his brother once parted, commemorated in verse:"Ascending high, I gaze back at undulating slopes; Where only rooftops emerge and vanish like boats." This was the suburban periphery of Guancheng during the Northern Song Dynasty. To preserve the old city's vanishing memory, the editors painstakingly compiled this series, including Old City Deities—which meticulously documents seasonal temple fairs. The Fire God Temple Fair, a Zhengzhou tradition held annually on the 7th day of the first lunar month near the intersection of Shuyuan Street and Bo'ai Street, exemplifies these vibrant folk customs. The northeast corner of this intersection originally housed a three-bay temple enshrining clay deities, its walls adorned with painted divine tablets. The Fire God Temple Fair traces its origins to ancient fire deity worship. The series also documents other temple fairs—the Ox King Fair, Three Officials Fair, Qixi Festival Fair, and Huanggang Temple Buddha Fair—each meticulously presenting their historical roots, narrative traditions, ritual particularities, and taboos.

Old Streets documents thirty timeworn lanes of Zhengzhou—millennium-old thoroughfares, ancient city alleys, cultural corridors, and commercial port streets. Among them, Guancheng Street existed as early as the Shang Dynasty (1610 BC), when King Tang's capital Bo encompassed what is now old Zhengzhou. Over successive dynasties, figures like Zichan of Zhou, Lu Qun of Tang, Zeng Gongliang and Wang Ruoxu of Song, and Magistrate Wang of Qing all left their marks on Guancheng Street—a perpetual political axis of Zhengzhou's mercantile capital. Its drum tower, an eight-pillared, three-bay structure with dougong brackets and upturned eaves, once maintained dawn-to-dusk timekeeping through bells and drums. During the Republican era, Feng Yuxiang repurposed it as a public reading room for newspapers and books—a democratic enlightenment project. Tragically, these cultural signposts have since vanished.

Old Shops chronicles Zhengzhou's culinary heritage, featuring establishments like Cai's Restaurant, Ge's Braised Pancake, He's Noodle House, Ma Yuxing, and Lixing Bakery—still thriving across the city's streets today. These iconic eateries have become must-try destinations for visitors, embodying Zhengzhou's gastronomic identity. The text records that Cai Shijun, founder of Capital Cai's Restaurant, hailed from Changyuan—a renowned cradle of Henan chefs. Selected as an imperial cook during the late Qing Xuantong reign, he established "Capital Cai's Old Wonton House" on the east side of West Second Street, Laofengang after the dynasty's collapse, later passing the legacy to his son Cai Yongquan. Cai's steamed dumplings garnered acclaim across eras: drawing Peking opera master Mei Lanfang in 1958, serving Chairman Mao in 1959, and inspiring Hong Kong gourmet Chua Lam's 2001 pilgrimage, who later penned in *Next Magazine*'s culinary column "*Feasting on Central Plains*":

> The towering bamboo steamer is lined with long Masson pine needles—previously steeped in rich broth and oil. Upon this fragrant bed rest the dumplings: wrappers thin as Cantonese wonton skins, pleated with twelve leaf-like folds, their broth-filled fillings remaining intact despite prolonged steaming. Layered flat atop the pine, they yield no spilled soup when lifted with chopsticks—until that first revelatory bite. Ah! That kaleidoscopic flavor—infused with pine resin's aroma—stands unequivocally as the supreme dumpling of my sixty years. All others pale in comparison, relegated to oblivion. While ancients battled for the Central Plains, I lack warlike urges—yet for this steamer of perfection, I'd wage culinary war without remorse!"[①]

① Meng Xianming, ed. *Pictorial Old Zhengzhou: Old Shops*. Zhengzhou: Zhongzhou Ancient Books Publishing House, 2004, p. 12.

Similarly, Ge's Braised Pancake—a Zhengzhou time-honored brand established in 1926—was designated "China's Famous Snack" during the inaugural national culinary appraisal and remains a beloved dining spot for locals and visitors alike. These historical records drawn from local gazetteers and literary recollections of bygone cityscapes form an intertextual network, collectively enriching Zhengzhou's urban memory.

Old Crafts documents Zhengzhou's carpenters, masons, painters, and cobblers, alongside noodle workshops, oil presses, tofu mills, seamstresses, and cart drivers. *Old Landmarks* chronicles urban heritage like the Neolithic Daha Village ruins, Ming-Qing city walls, the legendary Xishan Yellow Emperor site, Confucian and City God temples, and the historic Jialu River. Together, these works preserve both the human hands that shaped Zhengzhou and the ancient landscapes that anchored its civilization across millennia. The anthology *Old Folkways* compiles Zhengzhou's oral traditions—songs of wealth and poverty, "Nine Nines" winter chants, New Year ballads, and dragon worship hymns, alongside local proverbs. Its companion volume *Old Fare* meticulously catalogs the city's everyday foods, seasonal delicacies, festive dishes, and regional specialties. Meanwhile, *Old Verses* gathers literary tributes to the mercantile capital across dynasties, including: King Tang's "*Mulberry Grove Prayer*", Lü Yijian's "*Fubo Pavilion in Zhengzhou*", Zu Yong's "*Passing Through Zhengzhou*", Wang Wei's "*Lodging in Zhengzhou*", Su Shi's "*Horseback Verse for Zhengzhou*", Han Yu's "*Crossing Honggou*", Shen Quan's "*Ascending Guangwu Mountain*", and Li

Shangyin's "*Sunset Tower*"—each poem a palimpsestic layer in Zhengzhou's cultural stratigraphy.

Unlike the documentary and archival approach of *Pictorial Old Zhengzhou*, the Kaifeng-focused volume *Old Kaifeng: Urban Imagination and Cultural Memory* (Peking University Press, 2013) represents a scholarly interrogation of urban remembrance. Co-edited by Chen Pingyuan, David Der-wei Wang, and Guan Aihe, this academic treatise forms part of the "*Urban Imagination and Cultural Memory*" series, reframing historical materials through critical theory lenses. To the editors, "silent architecture, distant memories, rigorous documentation, exaggerated caricatures, bizarre legends, and ambiguous interpretations... all merit preservation and meticulous analysis. Unlike poets' laments, travelers' nostalgia, or activists' polemics, academic reconstructions of once-vibrant 'urban life'—methodical, objective—may lack dramatic flair, yet they form essential passageways to historical understanding and futuristic imagination, demanding our full intellectual engagement."[①] The volume includes seminal essays such as Zhao Yuan's "*Kaifeng: Water, Folkways, and Figures*", Zeng Yongyi's "*Investigating Northern Song Bianjing's Variety Theater*", Chen Pingyuan's "*Reluctant to Fade into Silence: The 'Kaifeng Narratives' of Zhang Changgong and Zhang Yigong*", and Mei Jialing's "*The City, an Empty Vessel? Kaifeng and Contemporary Female Bildungsromans*"—each excavating distinct strata of the

---

① Chen Pingyuan, David Der-wei Wang, and Guan Aihe, eds. *Kaifeng: Urban Imagination and Cultural Memory*. Beijing: Peking University Press, 2013, p. 2.

ancient capital’s cultural memory.

Among these, Liu Chunying’s “*Unveiling Kaifeng’s City Beneath the City: Historical Evolution and Archaeological Research of Ancient Kaifeng*” reveals through extensive excavations that “six stratified cities lie buried beneath modern Kaifeng: the Warring States-era Daliang (Wei Kingdom), Tang Dynasty’s Bianzhou, Five Dynasties/Northern Song’s Dongjing, Jin Dynasty’s Bianjing, Ming’s Kaifeng, and Qing’s Kaifeng—each successive settlement vertically stacked in chronological order within the geological strata.”[①] Li Yang’s “*Imperial Dreams and Alleyway Intimacies: Chinese Narratives in <Along the River During the Qingming Festival>*“ posits: “Pre-Song urbanism merely projected imperial power. Ancient capitals radiated from palace cores—walled enclaves evolving into ritual architectures of ‘Ancestral Left, Altars Right,’ compressing ‘all under heaven’ into ideological cityscapes. Through this ceremonial urbanism, material authority transmuted into liturgical sovereignty. The Song Dynasty’s urban breakthrough lay in initiating this secularization process. The emerging ‘alleyway culture’ embodied mature urban and commercial civilizations. With the ward system’s collapse, the traditional segregation of residential and commercial districts dissolved—evening drumbeats no longer imposed curfews, as the Song administration permitted citywide shop establishments and flourishing night

① Chen Pingyuan, David Der-wei Wang, and Guan Aihe, eds. *Kaifeng: Urban Imagination and Cultural Memory*. Beijing: Peking University Press, 2013, p. 15.

markets. As aristocratic privileges waned, cultural and status disparities narrowed, fostering a radically new civic sphere." "If earlier Chinese imaginaries contained only the 'Empire,' then *Along the River During the Qingming Festival* reveals the alleyway world—and crucially, their symbiotic fusion."①

As Mike Crang asserts: "Fiction may harbor deeper urban truths. We must transcend treating it merely as a documentary source—cities aren't just story backdrops, but geographic descriptions that encode social consciousness. ... The crux lies not in faithfully reproducing urban life, but in articulating the meanings of cityscapes."② Thus, cities and literature exist in a dialectical symbiosis: literary representations enable urban spaces to transcend their materiality, constructing in the realm of language a distinct cityscape born of textual imagination. "While literature imbues cities with imagined realities, urban transformations reciprocally reshape literary texts." Cities, literature, writers, and inhabitants exist in a complex constructive relationship—studying which facilitates the reclamation of meaning in our world.

---

① Chen Pingyuan, David Der-wei Wang, and Guan Aihe, eds. *Kaifeng: Urban Imagination and Cultural Memory*. Beijing: Peking University Press, 2013, pp. 476-477.

② Mike Crang, *Cultural Geography*, trans. Yang Shuhua and Song Huimin. Nanjing: Nanjing University Press, 2003, p. 50.

Chapter 6
Live Conditions: The Eroticized Urban Spectacle

Jean Baudrillard's theorization of contemporary society as "consumer society" underpins the secularization of cultural forms like literature and art. The material precondition for this societal shift lies in the "abundance" of commodities, where commercialization constitutes its fundamental logic and semiotic manipulation its operative core—culminating in a fetishistic ideology of consumption.[①] "The essence of consumer culture lies in perpetually multiplying semiotic, spectacular, and phantasmic commodities beyond basic human needs—thereby propelling cultural activity from mere survival, reproduction, and security toward communication, experience, and fantasy."[②] Within this consumerist paradigm, the textualization of reality's encroachment on daily life emerges as a critical concern, while writers, through their idiosyncratic sensibilities and imagistic frameworks, delineate pluralized urban landscapes. Under the overarching framework of consumer society, how textualized realities permeate everyday life has emerged as a critical inquiry, while writers—through their idiosyncratic perceptual modes and imaginative frameworks—depict multilayered urban landscapes.

1. Housing as a Social Dilemma

Jiao Shu's *House, House* (Writer's Publishing House, 2011) confronts

① Baudrillard, Jean. *La société de consommation* [*The Consumer Society*]. trans. by Liu Chengfu and Quang Zhigang. Nanjing: Nanjing University Press, 2006, p. 32, 85.

② Gao Xiaokang. "The Consumerist Nature and Epochal Characteristics of Contemporary Aesthetic Culture." Academic Research, no. 3, 2006.

the existential crises inflicted on ordinary citizens by China's decade-long property market surge. Through microcosmic narratives that interweave developers, government actors, and residents, the novel excavates the systemic roots of this inflationary frenzy while interrogating its human costs. The author portrays an earnest, morally upright young protagonist whose marriage plans—and ultimately, life trajectory—are derailed by unaffordable housing. This systemic predicament reduces personal aspirations to directionless struggles, leaving him adrift in existential paralysis. Even such exceptionally driven individuals confront this generational quandary, their agency dwarfed by macroeconomic tides—like frail reeds against a tsunami. The narrative culminates in his self-emancipation through refusal: opting out of the soul-crushing race for home ownership altogether.

Ren Ning graduated in 2000 from a prestigious university—one of China's top institutions for civil engineering and bridge design—which secured him a position at Pingyuan Design Institute. By his third year, he achieved exceptional early promotion to engineer. Meanwhile, his peers plunged into the housing frenzy: scrambling for down payments and mortgage approvals.

Ren Ning, ever self-assured, dismissed the anxiety: "Why fret? Housing will only improve—better layouts, superior construction. Those speculators peddling 'price surge' hysteria? Mere charlatanism." His unshakable faith in the government and nation stemmed from a lifetime of ideal conditions—

from his privileged upbringing to elite education. How could one so institutionally nurtured doubt official assurances while succumbing to populist fearmongering?①

This idealistic, self-assured, and dynamic youth found himself battered and demoralized by the housing market—forever outrun by soaring prices. Yet even his defeat could not alter the relentless macroeconomic tide of property inflation.

When Ren Ning defiantly quit the housing market, sellers didn't lower prices despite countless others like him bowing out in frustration. On the contrary, prices spiraled uncontrollably—fueled inexplicably by those unfazed buyers who flashed stacks of cash for apartments, even whole buildings at a time. Rumor had it these were tycoons with nowhere else to park their excess wealth but in brick and mortar. As for those purchasing two or three units, they abound—but far more common are the small-time players: bit-part actors in this grand drama, scraping together down payments until exhausted, then bargaining with banks for mortgages that will squeeze them dry for 20-30 years through austerity-living. To own a home, they're drained of vitality, their future selves—spiritually and materially—devoured by the twin demons of property and debt.②

Indeed, the grotesque realities depicted in the book mirror a widespread

① Jiao Shu. *House, House*. Beijing: Writer's Publishing House, 2011, p. 2.

② Jiao Shu. *House, House*. Beijing: Writer's Publishing House, 2011, p. 87.

societal malaise—since the new millennium, real estate's runaway gallop has gripped the nation's psyche. As National Bureau of Statistics data reveals, from January to November 2003, *national housing prices surged 4.6% year-on-year*, with Beijing's increase nearly a full percentage point higher. According to economists' analyses, China witnessed breakneck housing price surges in the past decade. Nationally, between 2001-2010, inflation-adjusted prices skyrocketed 130%, with a 39% increase from 2001-2005 and a further 66% leap from 2005-2010. ... This housing price surge paralleled breakneck urbanization. As the *China Statistical Yearbook 2011* documents, China's urban population share exploded from 17.92% (1978) to 49.95% (2010).① Amid the sweeping transformations of China's real estate market, Zhengzhou experienced its own dramatic housing price surge. As statistics reveal, the city's per-square-meter housing prices skyrocketed from ¥4,863 in 2007 to ¥13,218 in 2017 - a staggering increase that translates to an ¥840,000 total price jump for a standard 100-square-meter apartment over the decade. This relentless appreciation breaks down to an ¥84,000 annual increase, ¥7,000 monthly rise, ¥233 daily climb, and even an ¥10 hourly increment.② Behind these cold statistics lie countless stories of desperate home-seekers—partic-

① Lu Ming, Ou Haijun, and Chen Binkai. "Rationality or Bubble: An Empirical Study on Urbanization, Migration, and Housing Prices." The Journal of World Economy, no. 1, 2014.

② "Statistics Reveal: Zhengzhou Housing Prices Rose ¥10 Per Hour Over a Decade! What Can First-Time Buyers Do?". http://suzhou.jiwu.com/news/2840333.html

ularly young people crushed under housing prices that outpace their livelihoods. In *House, House*, Jiao Shu investigates the devastating impact of soaring prices on ordinary youth, while exposing the collusion between developers and local governments that fueled this runaway market. His work stands as a searing indictment of systemic failures and a sobering reflection on their human cost.

Similarly, Qiao Ye's nonfiction novel *Demolition Chronicle* tackles the incendiary issue of urban demolition, using investigative fieldwork to reconstruct events as "a microscopically detailed human specimen—a uniquely vivid social archive." The narrative unfolds in Zhang Village—my sister's hometown and a soon-to-be annex of the city's high-tech zone. Eager to maximize compensation before land expropriation, my sister and fellow villagers raced to erect illegal structures, with me serving as their clandestine strategist. Yet the completed buildings met with government countermeasures that swiftly fractured the villagers' united front. Through this episode, the author confronts the moral quandaries faced when self-interest collides with systemic power.

The narrative opens with "The Building Chronicle":

*Years ago, when city plans confirmed Future Road would cut through Zhang Village, sparking rumors of mass relocation, my foresighted sister immediately drained her savings—even borrowed ¥30,000 from me—to rotate her main house 180 degrees, rebuilding it as a two-story, south-facing structure. The ground floor became their home, the second floor a rental unit. Gradually, she expanded—adding a storage room, bathroom, and kitchen to the front yard—until a 6m×16m courtyard took shape. Thus did the dim, cramped tile-roofed house metamorphose into an auspicious modern dwelling. Each visit, seeing lush vegetables thriving in that yard, I'm tempted to rewrite Hai Zi's verse: "Facing my sister's house, spring's warmth blooms."[①] Yet this meticulously crafted house wasn't meant for living—but for demolition, a speculative vessel designed to extract maximum government compensation. The scheme: invest ¥60,000 - 70,000 to reap ¥240,000 - 250,000 in pure profit. The story's second act becomes a tactical duel between officials and villagers, where the ultimate victor emerges as GDP itself. "Say what you will, these demolitions have supercharged our local economy—spectacularly! The endless cycle of raze-and-rebuild keeps half the town employed. *Floor-tilers now pull ¥500 daily*! Even my diner's thriving—all thanks to the demolition boom."

Indeed, urbanization's relentless march has been paralleled by volumes of demolition chronicles. For displaced residents, the expropriation of ancestral lands represents not just material loss but emotional severance—rendering their compensation demands a perceived moral right, mirroring the national psyche of opportunistic maximization ("claim every advantage"). "The

① Qiao Ye. *Demolition Chronicle*. Zhengzhou: Henan Literature and Art Publishing House, 2012, 13–14.

emergence of 'nail households' in urban demolitions predominantly stems from dissatisfaction with compensation packages. Their resistance reflects both psychological deprivation and calculated profit-seeking—with most tactics aimed at securing greater payouts. While these holdouts employ bold strategies, they represent a tiny minority; the vast majority remain silent casualties of relocation."① This precisely mirrors the sisters in Qiao Ye's Demolition Chronicle—their tactical alliances and counter-maneuvers ultimately ending in defeat.

Since the 1998 commercialization of housing, residential property has remained a burning social issue. In the 12 years preceding this reform, annual commercial housing sales hovered below 100 million square meters—with only a *modest 10-million-sqm surge* in 1992, likely spurred by Comrade Deng Xiaoping's Southern Tour. "A pivotal shift occurred in 1998 when housing monetization reforms took effect: residential commercial housing sales first exceeded 100 million square meters, then quadrupled in just four years to 237 million (2002). Post-2008's ¥4 trillion stimulus, 2009 saw a meteoric rebound to 862 million. By 2013, sales shattered the 1 billion threshold, reaching 1.157 billion square meters."② Writers' engagement with this do-

① Chen Shaojun and Liu Yuzhen. "The Game Theory Logic of 'Nail Households' in Urban Housing Demolitions: A Case Study of Displaced Residents in N City." Dongjiang Journal, no. 1, 2011.

② Yang Guoming. *The Past and Present of China's Housing Commercialization*. http://blog.sina.com.cn/s/blog_49a802270101jk9a.html

main reflects an isomorphic relationship with urbanization itself—their observational acuity and critical reflections collectively composing vibrant social histories in literary form.

2. New Emotional Topographies

Among Henan writers, Yang Dongming and Sun Yu stand out for their nuanced portrayals of urban emotional landscapes. Yang probes the philosophical dimensions of sexuality, while Sun maps women's affective and existential terrains—together charting the psychogeography of rapid urbanization.

Yang Dongming, a pioneer in chronicling urban emotional and psychological states, authored numerous "Speculative Eros" novels—his city-as-text series. The Too-Great Problem opens with a preamble framing the commodified urban spectacle, set in the fictional Huangyang City.

Anya Community's renown stems not from luxury condos—unlike villa-studded enclaves, its twenty-odd six-story apartments epitomize modest urban living. Its fame springs from pioneering European-style lawns and ornamental fencing: palace-guard spear-like railings crowned with *18th-century-style carriage lanterns* at intervals, evoking aristocratic processionals.[1]

---

[1] Yang Dongming. *The Too-Great Problem*. Zhengzhou: Henan Literature and Art Publishing House, 2001, p. 1.

The narrative unfolds around an extramarital affair. Qiao Guo—a striking urban professional enduring relentless workplace harassment—maintains principled resistance until unwittingly entangled in illicit passion. Tormented by guilt toward her husband and child, yet she was unable to sever the emotional bond.

The necessity of weaving lies to deceive her husband filled Qiao Guo with self-loathing. Her sole consolation: this deception served love. But was it truly love? Yes—in every Lu Lianbi-less moment, she ached for him with bittersweet intensity, yearning yet dreading their encounters. Each farewell became a tearful internal vow: "This is the last time... the absolute last."

No—this wasn't love. Qiao Guo recognized the emotional palette of her longing: not joy's vibrancy, but oppression's gray hues. True love, she knew, should never taste of self-inflicted melancholy...①

To the author, love is more of a human game, a kind of novelty and excitement.

When Qiao Guo was dating her husband Ruan Weixiong, they too had frequent dates and went to the movies often. Holding hands and nestling together, they experienced a steady warmth and contentment—like sailing on a tranquil river, where the heart finds serene comfort. In stark contrast, her rendezvous with Lu Lianbi was charged with the novelty of first love and the

① Yang Dongming. *The Too-Great Problem*. Zhengzhou: Henan Literature and Art Publishing House, 2001, p. 120.

furtive thrill of secrecy. It felt like careening down winding mountain roads—jolting, stumbling, recklessly exhilarated...

Qiao Guo deemed herself "wicked" for such feelings—yet remained powerless to brake this careering emotional vehicle.[①]

The central narrative revolves around a woman and three men, with the author conducting meticulous emotional analysis. For Qiao Guo, her strongest attachment remains with her husband—a love encompassing him, their child, and their home, sustained by mutual devotion forged through shared hardships, unbreakable familial bonds, and inescapable social obligations that tightly bind them together. Yet she found no sexual fulfillment with her husband. With her lover Lu Lianbi, she experienced the primal joy of physical intimacy—humanity's instinctual pursuit. Her admirer Liu Renjie, meanwhile, offered a spiritual allure, transporting her to lyrical, picturesque realms. But drowning in these emotional entanglements, Qiao Guo symbolically emasculated her lover before choosing self-annihilation.

"*Who Withers for Whom*" (Writer's Publishing House, 2005) traces the life of urban woman Zhong Wenxin—kept in her youth, abandoned for infidelity, then ditched by her boyfriend, before finally falling for a male prostitute. The narrative explores virtual chatrooms as spaces of urban emotional

---

① Yang Dongming. *The Too-Great Problem*. Zhengzhou: Henan Literature and Art Publishing House, 2001, p. 139.

displacement, and wealthy but lonely women's intertwined yearnings for intimacy and sex. The male protagonist Shi Dachuan, a rural-born schoolteacher, refuses his father's impoverished fate after glimpsing wider horizons. "The city's bustling commercial streets taught him what wealth and status meant; its neon-lit dance halls revealed carefree pleasure; its extravagant banquets demonstrated luxurious indulgence; and its gated villas showcased an entirely different life..." Eventually buckling under family burdens and personal vanity, he chose to become a male escort—performing his "companion" role with professional diligence.

For the female protagonist Zhong Wenxin, her life unfolds as an unrelenting tragedy: seduced by her superior in youth, kept as a mistress by a Taiwanese businessman, she falls for piano teacher Han Bing—only to see him lose an eye to the businessman's brutal retaliation when their affair is exposed. Abandoned by both Han Bing and the businessman, she conceives a child with the family's male servant in her most vulnerable state. Years later, her daughter's persistent search for her father invites mockery from the businessman's family and cold rejection from Han Bing. Yet her biological father—deemed too socially inferior by Zhong Wenxin—remains perpetually obscured, driving her daughter into psychological turmoil. Meanwhile, Zhong herself clings to male prostitute Shi Dachuan, whose uncanny resemblance to Han Bing rekindles her obsession. She bankrolls their relationship, even as it retraumatizes her daughter.

Rejecting Romance (Writer's Publishing House, 1997) follows young entrepreneur Chu Feng—outwardly successful yet tormented by unspeakable family horrors. His father Chu Zhengren, overwhelmed by his wife's paralysis, rapes their young niece Xiuxiu, the live-in maid, initiating years of coerced relations. After Xiuxiu's marriage, harassed beyond endurance, she murders Chu Zhengren with a venomous snake. To protect his public image, Chu Feng manipulates Xiuxiu into suicide, silencing the truth. Wife Wei Yimei, misreading her husband's fidelity, embarks on an affair that culminates in divorce. Chu Feng later meets kindred spirit Meng Xian, a television producer, yet opts to marry well-connected Beijing socialite Li Yaya. Their kisses feel like corporate handshakes—this power alliance, though loveless, thrives on ruthless synergy. When Meng asks "As an entrepreneur, what do you seek in life?" Chu Feng replies coldly: "Success. The intoxicating rush of achievement. This era has no use for romance—you must spurn it, steeling yourself to march step-by-step toward success."[①] Yet the story concludes with an ironic twist: the accomplished entrepreneur Chu Feng, exhausted by his triumphs, wonders if he shouldn't indulge with his mistress after all. Thus, urban love's ephemerality, ruthless careerism, and matrimonial fragility coalesce into the quintessential metropolis malaise.

For Yang Dongming, his work persistently dissects urban psyches, em-

---

① Yang Dongming. *Rejecting Romance*. Beijing: Writer's Publishing House, 1997, p. 322.

ploying psychological realism to trace how lived experiences shape behavioral patterns and inner journeys. Take Madam Cai in The *Too-Great Problem*: this reclusive elderly woman, upon overhearing illicit intimacies, repeatedly exposes the affair to Lu Lianbi's wife—driven by jealousy toward younger women and her own festering bitterness. In *Rejecting Romance*, Chu Zhengren—though a rapist who long exploited his wife's niece Xiuxiu—rationalizes his crimes through his wife's paralysis and dead marital bed. When Xiuxiu escapes via marriage, he's gutted by loss. In the kitchen, visions haunt him: "Xiuxiu's bowed head over the sink... Her warmth lingering on knife handles, fingerprints on dish rims... Even cooking oil conjures her oil-scented skin." He became a sleepwalking specter, haunting Xiuxiu with obsessive visits. Meanwhile, Xiuxiu's festering hatred crystallized into a lethal equation: "If he ruins me, I'll erase him." This psychologically exacting portrayal—where every action follows emotional calculus—reveals Yang's mastery of criminal interiority.

Sun Yu's women's fiction series—*Don't Touch My Bed* (Beijing Masses Publishing House, 2010)—excavates urban women's clandestine emotional worlds, chronicling phenomena like: being the "other woman" in youth, amassing wealth, then hiring male escorts as affluent divorcées seeking carnal-emotional release. These narratives unveil the city's shadow geographies, exposing social grotesqueries through female audacity.

Don't Touch My 'Bed' depicts Hao Min, who suspects her husband's infidelity yet obsessively maintains marital appearances. She battles the urge to snoop through Xiao Naxin's phone, but "peeking becomes an addiction—once Pandora's box is opened, the descent is irreversible." Gradually, Hao Min escalates her surveillance: rifling through his wallet, pockets, and luggage, even sniffing his underwear for tell-tale traces of other women.① Under such oppressive living conditions, the relationship between the couple grew increasingly polite yet distant, their meticulously maintained marriage constantly on the verge of collapse. Yet Hao Min still tried to console herself: "If I don't stay here, where else can I go? Back to my parents' home? A married daughter is like spilled water—wouldn't it be humiliating for a woman my age to return in defeat?"②

Sleeping in Clothes presents a seemingly beautiful and pure "older woman-younger man romance", yet even this cannot withstand the crushing weight of money. Jiang Mingsheng, who claimed to love "me" for so many years, ultimately abandoned "me" under the overwhelming temptation of a wealthy Hong Kong woman's promises—and his own desperate need for a fresh start to success. At their parting, he even recited poetic farewells over the phone, declaring with performative tenderness: "I will always remember your birthday. Every year, on that day, you will be the first to receive my blessings, no matter where I am in the world." The fragility of emotions in

---

① Sun Yu: *Please Don't Touch My "Bed"*, Masses Publishing House, 2010, p. 43.

② Sun Yu: *Please Don't Touch My "Bed"*, Masses Publishing House, 2010, p. 45.

the face of money taught "me" a harsh lesson in social reality.

The Hollow Bed (China Overseas Chinese Publishing House, 2010) depicts the emotional life of urban woman Su Mei—a trajectory of transactional relationships. In her youth, she was kept by Chen Mu, a powerful older man, in an exchange of mutual convenience. Later, having achieved financial success, she herself chooses to patronize a high-end male escort, indulging in his youthful body—only to be swindled out of her fortune by the morally bankrupt Zhang Yadong. Ultimately, she and the male escort cling to each other for survival, a hollow echo of intimacy. In Su Mei's life, as long as emotions and interests remained unrelated, everything was sustained perfectly. Faced with Chen Mu—a man even older than her father—she carefully performed her role, feigning affection and catering to his every whim. "She felt she had fully immersed herself in the character—to act convincingly, she had to not only embody the role but also win the audience's approval, drawing them into the plot. Only then could she be considered a good actress." Chen Mu, of course, saw through Su Mei's act. He understood all too well that her devotion was never truly for him alone. "At his age, he knew exactly how it worked: 'How deep is my love for you?' was just another way of asking, 'How much money do you have?'"[①] In her later years, Su Mei also sought pleasure—and discovered that money could buy men. A monthly fee of 100,000 yuan was no issue for her, yet that very number left a bitter aftertaste

① Sun Yu: *The Hollow Bed*, China Overseas Chinese Publishing House, 2011, p. 29.

from last night's escapade. But she could just as quickly shrug it off: What did it matter? She could casually keep flowers, pets, or men, and when in the mood, even fling away fortunes in charity. It was, after all, a kind of joy. Yet this condescending happiness was short-lived. After her bankruptcy, the very male escort whose dignity she had once trampled chose to take her in—not without delivering a crushing blow: "Director Su, don't fool yourself into thinking you're noble. Especially not a woman past fifty, penniless."

In this work, the author introduces another female character—Xu Yanqiu, Su Mei's live-in maid. A rural migrant, she embodies the traditional virtues of country women: simplicity and diligence. Yet despite her innate honesty, she develops a deep bond of trust with her employer, Su Mei, who sponsors her education in finance and secures her a position in the company. However, under the manipulative influence of the conman Zhang Yadong, Xu Yanqiu is seduced and coerced into embezzlement—a betrayal that ultimately triggers Su Mei's financial ruin and suicide. The author probes the psychological motivations behind Xu Yanqiu's downfall—a toxic interplay of female jealousy and Zhang Yadong's emotional manipulation. She covets Su Mei's elegant clothes and romantic relationships, these burning envies becoming the catalyst for her moral unraveling. Though ostensibly a success story—a maid rising to white-collar status—the narrative, through Zhang Yadong's urban gaze, exposes the city's contempt for her roots. Even when aware of her virginity, he contemptuously hands her a tattered rag to stanch the bleeding. Even when exploiting her emotional dependence, he never masks his disgust for her ineradicable "country stink"—those indelible marks of rural origin she neither recognizes nor can shed.

Sun Yu's two works both delve into the fraught emotional landscapes of urban women—infidelity, older woman-younger man relationships, extramarital affairs, kept arrangements, and transactional sex—using these relational fractures to dissect the fragile psyches beneath their seemingly empowered facades. Even in *Women Fabricated*, where the author attempts to construct a model of the "new new woman" through Zhuo Yiqin, the narrative exposes the hollowness of such aspirations. After nearly a decade struggling in the city, cycling through ten industries and relocating over a dozen times, Zhuo finally claws her way into the so-called "White-Bone-Elite" tier—white-collar, corporate backbone, elite—only to be trapped in the "virtuous cycle" of car loans and mortgage payments. Now, the latest manifesto of these so-called "new new women" has emerged: "Achieve the Nine Modernizations ASAP!" ①Figure: Devilish curves; ②Income: White-collar stability; ③Chores: Outsourced liberation; ④Happiness: Daily dopamine hits; ⑤Aesthetics: Petite bourgeoisie chic; ⑥Shopping: Unrestrained frenzy; ⑦ Romance: Perfunctory longevity; ⑧Lovers: Industrial-scale collection; ⑨ Husbands: Enslaved compliance.[①] This archetypal metropolitan woman, after cycling through affairs with married men, ultimately chooses sperm-donor parenthood—curating single motherhood like another lifestyle accessory.

---

① Sun Yu: *The Hollow Bed*, China Overseas Chinese Publishing House, 2011, p. 148.

Beneath their seemingly indomitable facades lies the inarticulable anguish of modern womanhood. Indeed, the prominence of marital anxiety, romantic anxiety, and age anxiety in contemporary literature reveals an unexpectedly acute cultural phenomenon. This trajectory traces back to Wang Anyi's "unconscious actors"—characters whose narratives opened floodgates for literary scrutiny of urban women's behaviors, psychologies, trajectories, and fates. Works like her novellas *Mi Ni* and *I Love Bill* deploy unsparing realism to portray women adrift in cities, ensnared in emotional whirlpools, their unconscious choices hurtling them toward tragedy. *Love and Money in Hong Kong* employs an unflinching lens to expose the transactional dynamics of affection in the market-reform era. A Shanghai woman arrives in Hong Kong, maintaining a cohabitation arrangement with the businessman Old Wei. Her singular goal is emigration, while he serves as both her transactional bargaining chip and a fleeting source of warmth. Eventually, their purposes fulfilled, they part ways without ceremony—geographically and emotionally severed.

Perhaps female authors are particularly inclined to lavish narrative attention on women's plights. Consider Shao Li's *Minghui's Christmas*: Minghui, a rural sex worker who migrates to the city, believes she has found stability—only to realize she can never penetrate the urban elite circles of her patron and ultimately chooses suicide. Or Qiao Ye's *I Truly Love You*: the elder sister, initially motivated by material necessity (paying her sister's tuition), becomes intoxicated by consumption, dragging the younger sibling into her wealth-accumulation schemes—even at the cost of the latter's love and autonomy. How should urban women's fates be written?—This ought to be a question. Are they merely the "second sex" or perpetual victims? In the relentless march of urbanization, must women who migrate to cities truly forfeit self-actualization? Must they inevitably surrender autonomy and dignity? The authors' sympathy for these destinies—and their humanitarian concern for the marginalized—is evident. Yet we yearn to witness greater reservoirs of spiritual resilience within these women themselves.

3. Desire and the Possibility of Breaking Free

In 2013, Mo Bai's novel *Desire* was published—a sprawling 570,000-word epic spanning three decades, divided into Red Volume, Yellow Volume, and Blue Volume. The narrative follows Tan Yu, Wu Xiyu, and Huang Qiuyu, three men born on the same day in the same village, their lives intertwined yet diverging. This deliberate coincidence serves as a narrative device to explore how individuals from shared origins "drown" in the vast ocean of desire. As the author states in the postscript: "The desire for power, the desire for flesh, the desire for survival—desire surges through us like a flood, an ocean that drowns countless lives. Some perish suffocated by desire, their selfhood and independent spirit never awakened." This novel's exploration stems from a fundamental inquiry into "the existential value of desire."① Indeed, the lit-

① Yu Hua: *Can I Trust Myself?*, People's Daily Press, 1998, p. 171.

erary depiction of desire became a defining feature of 1990s Chinese literature—from *Ruined City to I Love Dollars*, *A Private Life*, and *A War of One's Own*. These works transformed the portrayal of primal urges into a vital literary phenomenon, a liberation from ideological repression, while preserving seminal cross-sections of that historical moment. Yet Mo Bai's ambition extends far beyond this—he dedicates two decades of meticulous labor to intertwine his narrative of desire with the seismic shifts of a thirty-year era. To analyze Desire is to dissect how the author lays bare the cravings of an entire generation. In doing so, we uncover not only Mo Bai's profound meditation on human nature and existence, but also a vital key to understanding that generation's collective coming-of-age and spiritual odyssey.

Mo Bai's writing delves unflinchingly into the shadowed recesses of human nature. In his *Desire* trilogy, he articulates his literary ethos with striking clarity: "All of us with rural roots who migrate to cities face assaults on our dignity. Under the historic urban-rural binary policy, peasants were stripped of fundamental respect. Decades of systemic inequity bred in them a psychology of self-abasement." Now they have come to the city—their values, their moral compass, violently upended. Adrift, they grasp for footing. In China's long history, never before have so many peasants abandoned ancestral lands en masse. Ours is a society in tectonic transition, convulsing with psychic disarray. This turmoil stems doubly: from the material precarity of survival, and from a deeper spiritual dislocation.[①] Though Mo Bai consistently emphasizes his rural roots, his psychological experience as an intellectual migrant diverges sharply from that of peasant laborers. This distinction drives his deeper excavation of spiritual desolation. For him, "The city swells endlessly with these very desires—its air thick with the stench of coin, yet frigid and emotionally barren." Meanwhile, Sun Fangyou—who migrated to the city alongside Mo Bai—constructed small-town characters through realist brushstrokes. Mo Bai, however, remained obsessively committed to avant-garde writing. "Icy" might be the key to deciphering his literary world: a realm where warmth proves irrecoverable. Even in his works, the interactions between Tan Yu and his "scarlet muse" Ye Qiu—such as her close readings of his manuscripts or the literary salon she hosts for him—stand as rare oases of tenderness.

In the days that followed, many details of that literary salon faded from Tan Yu's memory... yet he secretly preened over his triumphant performance. That evening, he had spoken with raw vulnerability—recounting his origins, his hardships, even shedding unscripted tears so visceral they drew several young women into shared weeping. As they exited the academic building, Ye Qiu gripped his arm, trembling: "Brilliant... you were absolutely brilliant."...Ye Qiu's voice had dissolved into a melody that lingered in his senses. When they shook hands at parting, Tan Yu—under the cover of night—

---

① Meng Qingshu: Multidimensional Reflections on Fiction: An Interview with Mo Bai, Yunnan People's Publishing House, 2016, p. 32.

clutched her hand. One squeeze. Then another. That hand seemed to cease being flesh, becoming pure emotional current, a conduit of shared feeling. This remained Tan Yu's most indelible memory of that evening.[①]

Yet Ye Qiu, as an urban woman, embodies the city's value system—even while being portrayed as unworldly, having divorced her husband over his money-grubbing vulgarity. Her modernity reveals itself when she lectures Tan Yu: "Only a fool like you would still bury himself in scholarship. What era do you think this is? Who dedicates themselves to learning anymore? Look at what everyone else is doing—they're all scrambling for cash." "If you want to become somebody, you must sever your roots—take flight, leave it all behind! The baggage you carry is too heavy!" Even his closest confidant subscribed to this brutal logic. Tan Yu turned to poetry to voice his isolation, only to find "no words could capture this sorrow." In the end, he drowned in desire: divorcing his wife, tumbling into affairs with Xiaohui and Xiaohong—a reckless surrender to the self. The narrative traces an expanding web of characters consumed by their obsessions—from Wang Yang, Qian Dayong and Tan Yu drowning in avarice, to Wu Tianfu and Wu Xiyu shackled by thirst for fame, to the sexual compulsions binding Tan Yu, Xiaohui, Xiaohong, Yin Lin, Wu Xiyu, the "Five Nymphs", Huang Qiuyu and Mi Hui. Qian Dayong embodies performative craving while Zhao Jing and Yin Lin ache with confessional urgency. Yet it is erotic obsession that receives the

① Mo Bai: *Desire*, Hunan Literature & Art Publishing House, 2013, p. 121.

most lavish literary dissection—a primal force rendered in grotesquely exquisite detail.

For Wu Xiyu, Niu Wenzao—"that consummate frigid woman"—perpetually stranded him in the purgatory of unfulfilled desire. "For years, I've endured this exquisite torment," he lamented. Similarly, Huang Qiuyu's marital despair—his wife's emotional illiteracy—became the alibi for his philandering, draping his affairs in the gauze of humanistic justification. As sociologists starkly observe: "The thwarting of status-climbing desire doesn't merely force abandonment of material aspirations—it annihilates social dignity, leaving self-worth in ruins." "Lasswell has demonstrated that when the ideals of the 'successful self' are shattered and former convictions rendered meaningless, primal impulses turn inward—morphing into self-flagellation, devolving into masochistic or psychologically self-destructive debauchery."[①] Thus, Tan Yu divorced his wife. Beyond his entanglement with Ye Qiu, he plunged into reckless affairs with Xiaohui and Xiaohui, drowning in hedonism while agonizing: "What demon drives me here? Love? At nearly forty? Why this relentless hunger? Am I... a soul forever soiled?" Wu Xiyu, too, would drown himself in carnal abandon and Huang Qiuyu's endless romantic games. Though Mo Bai devoted himself to "avant-garde" writing—where avant-garde primarily denotes technique—the writer remains, fundamentally, a storyteller. This inevitably calls to mind his deliberate declaration in the

① Mannheim, Karl: Man and Society in an Age of Reconstruction: Studies in Modern Social Structure, translated by Zhang Lüping, Yilin Press, 2011, p. 84.

postscript: "Human dignity was the central question haunting me throughout *Desire*'s creation."

As is widely known, Mo Bai trained as a visual artist, possessing an innate sensitivity to chromatic symbolism—hence his trilogy's division into Red Volume, Yellow Volume, and Blue Volume. This evokes Wen Yiduo's canonical poem "Colors":

"Life was a blank sheet devoid of worth,

Till green granted growth, red passion's birth,

Yellow taught loyalty, blue moral grace,

Pink bestowed hope while grey draped sorrow's face.

As this polychrome portrait achieved its frame,

Black added death to complete the claim.

Since then I've doted on my mortal coil,

For I worship its colors—this vibrant toil."

In *Desire*, Mo Bai takes the three primary colors as his narrative axis, mixing from them the prismatic spectrum of human craving. The novel's essence lies in relentless complexity—each volume whispers to readers: "Reality outstrips your darkest imaginings." Here, desires and indulgences don't alleviate life's torment; they catalyze self-annihilation. Page after page lays bare the sorrows and deaths birthed by unrestrained wanting—a chromatic autopsy of appetite's wreckage. The novel opens with an unrelenting procession of death: Jin's grandmother passes, Jin commits suicide, her son Xiaoyu dies, Wang Binggui meets his end, a woman is killed in a car crash, Ji Chunyu's father dies, Ji Chunyu himself murders and is arrested, Tu Wenqing commits rape and murder, Yu Tianfu succumbs to cancer, the Seven Fairy's son is kidnapped and murdered, the Seven Fairy descends into madness and dies, Wu Xiyu is killed in a car accident, Huang Qiuyu is murdered, and Su Nan is left vegetative after another crash.

Alongside this carnage unfolds a tapestry of ruptured bonds: Lei Xiumei's marital strife, Xiaohui's parents' divorce, Tan Yu's divorce, Chen Hao's divorce, Ye Qiu's divorce, Wang Yang's divorce, Wu Xiyu's affair with Yin Lin, Niu Wenzao's mother's sex scandal, Yang Jinghuan's divorce theatrics, and Chen Xianzhi's marital collapse. And weaving through it all—madness: Jin's derangement, the Seven Fairy's insanity, Niu Wenzao's unraveling. Each tragedy, each fracture, each descent into delirium becomes a brushstroke in Mo Bai's grotesque fresco of desire's fallout.

This morally ambiguous, existentially oppressive narrative mode has been labeled "degree-zero writing" by some scholars—yet such categorization fails to encapsulate Mo Bai's relentless interrogation of human existence, his piercing scrutiny of the era, his unflinching historical reckoning. Within the text, he has Xiaohui confront Tan Yu with the devastating question: "What artifact could possibly encapsulate our age?" Woven throughout the historical narrative are deliberate insertions of seismic events: Liu Shaoqi's death, the Xinyang incident wrought by the Great Leap Forward, the AIDS epidemic, Almaty in Xinjiang, Yu Luoke's "On Family Origins", the "12 • 8" catastrophic accident, and the collapse of a monument. These strategically implanted historical fragments stand in stark relief against the nameless, mundane desires of individuals—a dissonance that lays bare the absurdity where grand history and private hunger intersect. Though the trilogy unfolds under the vivid banners of red, yellow, and blue, its foundation remains irrevocably gray—a monochrome of gloom where each character stumbles directionless toward ruin through their own cravings. Tan Yu can never return to his rural roots; Wu Xiyu's political ambitions die with him in a car crash; Huang Qiuyu meets a violent, untimely end.

The writer remains, above all, "the storyteller"—regardless of narrative form. Yet since the 1990s, China's three decades of metamorphosis have defied literary reconstruction. Critics diagnose this as "the impotence of engagement," where fractured social coherence—more than any authorial failing—has birthed what Yu Hua calls "our epoch of seismic disparities" and Yan Lianke declares "Reality's absurdity is now racing with writers' imaginations." The erratic, rapidly evolving social fabric has induced widespread discomfort. Writers' own lives are fractured—how to express such fragmented experiences becomes a perplexing challenge. This inevitably brings Mo Bai to mind: his arduous early years, his eventual migration to the city through writing, only to face the literary transformations of the 1990s. While many avant-garde writers, tempered by market forces and self-adjustment, returned to realist writing, Mo Bai stubbornly clung to avant-garde techniques, using dreams and memories to construct his literary world. "Loneliness" remains an inescapable theme throughout the Desire trilogy. Born in 1956, Mo Bai came of age during China's highly unified collective society. He shares a generational biography with contemporaries like Mo Yan and Yan Lianke - the indignity of hunger and survival struggles, the frustrations stemming from family "historical issues." Yet theirs was perhaps the most socially conscious generation, their births and growth structurally intertwined with the People's Republic. Even Wang Anyi, celebrated as the "heir to Shanghai-style literature" and most skilled at urban narratives, emphatically declares herself a "daughter of the Republic." Thus, their stories invariably carry profound societal consciousness. From this perspective, perhaps we can discern Mo Bai's endeavor—amidst the desire-saturated urban landscape—to establish "Yinghe Town" as his spiritual stronghold, striving to reconstruct a "psychic homeland."

From September 1980 to December 1991—a full eleven years and three months—this period of my life was spent at a primary school in my hometown. ...Now, before the summer sun has risen, the forest of urban buildings and the sea of green treetops are already driving up the temperature. The shuttling cars below and the distant chimneys spewing gray smoke make me feel increasingly distant from that tranquil rural life. How can I, in this society that worships money and power, reach the heart of those days—when material poverty coexisted with spiritual abundance?①

Here, the author frames the external world as a realm of money and power, while striving toward an inner ideal—a life of material simplicity yet spiritual plenitude. Modernization and urbanization represent both social progress and the simultaneous construction of capitalist logics, wealth accumulation, developmentalism, and rationalist thinking. For Mo Bai, "the fundamental task of literature must begin with the soul's self-examination and self-redemption."② In the narrative, the city—gray, unyielding, frigid—is swathed in desire and fear, leaving only the distant hometown as a warm sanctuary and idealized refuge. Thus, the author turns to dreamscapes, fantasies, and memory to excavate the sustaining power of spiritual self-sufficiency. "Authentic artworks—the true avant-garde of our era—never conceal this alienation between art and reality. They neither diminish nor bridge the divide, but amplify it, intensifying their own irreconcilability with the given world to such a degree that art renounces all practical utility. It is precisely through this refusal that art fulfills its epistemic function...compelling humanity to confront the dreams it has betrayed and the sins it has forgotten."③

---

① Mo Bai: *Birds and Dream Flight*, Henan Literature & Art Publishing House, 2016, p. 79.

② Mo Bai: *Dreamscapes, Fantasies and Memories*, Henan University Press, 2013, p. 416.

③ Dong Xuewen & Rong Wei: New Dimensions in Modern Aesthetics: Selected Essays on "Western Marxist" Aesthetics, Peking University Press, 1990, p. 255.

Thus, he employs the monumental yet heterogeneous *Desire* trilogy to articulate his literary vision—a prism refracting urbanity's all-consuming maw. Tan Yu's metamorphosis unfolds across this triptych: from *The Age of Streaking*'s protagonist (a rootless struggler severed from rural identity yet rejected by the city), to *Desire and Fear*'s detached observer, culminating in *Someone Else's Room* as Huang Qiuyu's truth-exhumer. Through this stereoscopic narrative architecture, Mo Bai constructs an entire generation's existential quagmire. The post-1990s Chinese society has inflicted profound psychic maladjustment upon a generation—whether from nostalgia for the 1980s' idealist fervor and humanist warmth, or the failed attempts to reconstruct collapsed spiritual worlds, or perhaps the sheer unspeakability of an absurd, fragmented reality. This dissonance inevitably complicates any engaged praxis with the present. Even in works that confront reality head-on—such as Yan Lianke's The Chronicles of Zhalie, which self-identifies as "mythorealism"—the approach remains deliberately oblique. Desire's engagement with our era proves elusive: its fragmented histories and opaque dreamscapes deliberately obscure the reader's gaze. Yet these shadowed narratives of craving coalesce into Mo Bai's essential thesis—the annihilation wrought by unrestrained desire. From Tan Yu's psychic collapse, to Wu Xiyu's vanishing without a trace, to Huang Qiuyu's violent demise—each constitutes a threnody of desire, a tragedy wrought by unbridled craving.

Chapter 7

The City as Backdrop: In Search of a Mode of Observation

For Baudelaire, the flâneur is one who "enters the city and its crowds to construct a private universe of meaning—observing yet never assimilating, cultivating irony and detachment as armor. This very stance of ironic alienation crowns the flâneur modernity's unlikely hero."① This archetype was hailed by Leo Ou-fan Lee as "the flâneur's sublime idol." Writing urban life comes naturally to China's post-New Era authors—their formative years coincided with urbanization's meteoric rise, their literary maturation mirroring the city's explosive growth. Capturing urban psychogeographies and metropolitan metamorphosis thus became central to their practice. Globalization granted them fluency in navigating cultural multiplicity while deepening their critical engagement with modernity's structural paradoxes. In *Invisible Cities*, Italo Calvino adopts the voice of an ancient envoy to articulate modernity's urban condition: "The endless city sprawls beyond comprehension, its scale dwarfing human perception—this is the metropolis as ungovernable leviathan." Such is the alienated urbanity of postindustrial society, a perpetually self-replicating phenomenon. Herein emerges literature's urgent mandate: to devise new optics for seeing the city anew.

1. The Flâneur and *Sparrow Dialogues*

Walter Benjamin observed: "One gets lost in cities as one gets lost in

① KeithTester. *The Flaneur*. London: Routledge. 1994. P7.

forests." Hence, his oeuvre teems with flâneurs—urban wanderers who navigate streets with psychic detachment, their alienation paradoxically sharpening observational acuity. Xi Tongfa's Sparrow Dialogues (a 2016 novella collection from Henan Literature & Art Publishing House) extends this tradition, framing urban youth through a similar lens of critical spectatorship. The novella Each Other dissects the gravitational weight of metropolitan existence on young lives. "Today's city is hijacked by material lust—genuine ease and smiles grow rare, especially among strangers passing on the streets. For many, a smile no longer signals joy or levity, but has become mere social mime, a mandatory performative mask."①

Zou Xiaoliang, an intern journalist, was abruptly dismissed by the editorial director after three months of diligent work. For him, journalism had become intolerably mundane—"shooting flags on National Day, mooncakes during Mid-Autumn Festival, zongzi for Dragon Boat Festival." "Media professionals spend their days safeguarding others' rights, yet when their own are violated, they stand powerless." Fuming, he stormed into a department store near the newspaper office. Dong Zhen'ou, a police officer with barely six months on the force, faced his own disillusionment: "The precinct's mired in petty cases—when not loaned out as ceremonial props for visiting officials, we're human barricades at soccer matches or pop concerts." This life felt like a colossal waste of youth—yet it was a career his shopkeeper parents had

① Xi Tongfa: *Sparrow Dialogues*, Henan Literature & Art Publishing House, 2016, p. 3.

begged and scraped to secure for him. After the police chief screamed at him with generational vendetta-like fury, he "flung his police cap—'Screw this! I'm done playing servant!'"—his mind blank as he mechanically turned toward the familiar mall. Erhuang worked at a construction site—physically slight and armed only with a community college diploma, he survived on his crew's charity. Wracked with guilt over his meager contributions, he repaid their kindness by volunteering as the sacrificial lamb to confront their boss over a year's worth of unpaid wages. Feng Jun, a contractor, hardly lived the ostentatious life one might expect. "Ordinary folks stash their savings in banks—we've got none. Every penny's sunk into construction sites, plus we're constantly borrowing from banks or investment firms. Truth is, the moment you 'become rich,' you're instantly impoverished." For him, the daily extravagant banquets at upscale hotels grew nauseating—"My mind's crammed with deals to discuss, favors to broker, fires to put out." With unpaid project funds dangling over him, Feng Jun couldn't even rant and rave like the migrant workers—he was trapped in a double bind: chasing developers for payment while dodging his own workers' wage demands. Sleepless nights left him drenched in cold sweats. To his daughter Feng Xiaoni, he was a perennial no-show, missing every birthday—until her eighth, when he finally took her to the mall for a gift... only to encounter Erhuang, who'd been lying in wait.

Thus, all converging lives collided in the mall—Erhuang seized the little girl, aiming to extort Contractor Feng. "To out-scoundrel a scoundrel," he reasoned. Officer Dong Zhen'ou, poised to leave, found himself cartwheeling through the air—an accidental hero crashing onto the assailant, his unintentional heroics celebrated as a hostage rescue. Meanwhile, the loafing journalist—camera in hand—captured the entire scene. The next day, two full pages of visual storytelling chronicled Dong's "heroic rescue" in meticulous timeline format. The absurdity was theatrical: lives spinning helplessly in their own orbits until a random convergence altered fate. The officer went from yesterday's resignation to today's hero—a grim parody of upward mobility. As for the true tragic figures? Their lives derailed onto unforeseen tracks.

The narrative's meticulous architecture lays bare urban discourse flattened by materialism into caricatures. Yet this story pierces deeper, mapping its characters' interior landscapes—their struggles, downfalls, rebellions, and the gnawing paralysis of being trapped in cities with no exits. Every fissure of despair is rendered with surgical precision. Each character carries their own untold histories, private agonies, and shrinking inner worlds beneath the city's glossy veneer—rehumanizing urban dwellers by laying bare their existential awkwardness.

In Life Goes On, the narrative traces a metropolitan spinster's romantic odyssey. During her grad school years, a budding romance collapsed when the man's mercenary mindset made the relationship untenable, forcing her to walk away. She never anticipated the man would "slap a ledger and a pile of receipts between them." Enraged, she "yanked a wad of cash from her handbag and hurled it onto the table without counting." The man speed-counted the bills, then snapped: "Short. Still owe me." These jaw-dropping, absurdist scenes—rendered with documentary realism—gain credibility through their economics-major backstory: the man rationalized her emotional demands as "sunk costs... non-recoupable per economic theory..." Lofty theoretical frameworks and self-consistent academic logic offered little solace. Perhaps disillusioned with love—or crushed under competitive pressures—she plunged into work, leaving no bandwidth for romance. By twenty-nine and a half, anxiety drove her to a "marriage factory." Yet even with her economics training, she "collapsed utterly when life's brutal equations demanded payment—defenseless against their relentless arithmetic. Despair—utter, suffocating despair." Before life's onslaught, even love becomes a luxury good: either a ROI-calculated transaction or assembly-line matchmaking at the marriage factory. This illusion of order and control lays bare emotion's pathetic impotence—a soul-crushing revelation.

No Time, Too Busy dissects urban existence—how its denizens seek solace in the flickering catharsis of virtual spaces. Crushed under multilayered pressures (existential, romantic, familial, professional), people grow isolated beyond words, transforming the digital realm into their confessional booth. The city-dweller's daily grind—the weight of survival, love, filial duty, speech, labor, income, household, peers, and position—compounds into an unsustainable load, leaving them spiritually bankrupt.. And with this burden comes an isolation so acute it deafens.

Loneliness springs from the rupture of social values. "Traditional societies operated with ordered hierarchies—clear binaries of good/evil. Modernity, by contrast, drowns us in chaotic, ambiguous, fractured value systems. To flee this uncertainty, people cling to their own dogmas, imposing personal frameworks to reconstruct familiar order. Yet they simultaneously reject others' imposed values—breeding mutual antagonism and alienation. Thus: isolation."① Here we observe how in *Fireworks*, even love proves ephemeral—reduced to wispy nostalgia. Yet this very loneliness embodies a double alienation: the solipsism of personal perception clashing with the city's relentless differentiation, which renders all experience uncannily strange. In *Fireworks*, the narrator voices bewilderment at metropolitan women: "Today's urban girls grew up alongside boys in kindergarten—male presence is mundane. With Super Girl-style androgyny setting trends, many no longer grasp how to perform girlhood. They chop hair short for efficiency, sacrificing waterfall tresses that once stirred hearts. They bro-fist boys, call them 'dude,' slap shoulders—just one of the guys* in cargo shorts and sneakers, their wardrobes deliberately degendered. Where, then, does elegance dwell? Where demureness?"② Thus, these narratives lay bare a mutual incomprehension: men

---

① Zhang Zhizhong & Wu Dengfeng: "*The Lonely Urban Forest: A Study of Xu Yi's Fiction*", in Literary Debates, No. 2, 2008.

② Xi Tongfa: *Sparrow Dialogues*, Henan Literature & Art Publishing House, 2016, p. 69.

bewildered by feminine aesthetics, women stunned by men's ruthless economization of love. Trapped in this dialogue of the deaf, individuals retreat into interior fortresses or digital facsimiles of intimacy—staging love stories fraught with performative authenticity.

Xi Tongfa, a seasoned journalist immersed in frontline reporting, possesses an anthropologist's grasp of social textures and a novelist's penetration of psyches. His stories—hovering between documentary and fiction—sketch urban ethnographic portraits: ordinary reporters, civil servants, migrant laborers, nouveau riche tycoons, and glossy-collar professionals. Yet his true focus pierces beyond professional façades to expose the unvarnished selves beneath. Through these vignettes of urban life, he strips away the city's glossy veneer to reveal its raw underbelly—while probing modernity's existential quandary: Where does the urban soul belong?

2. "Our Seven Halls and Eight Departments"

Nan Feiyan, an early standout among "post-80s" writers, debuted in high school with the novel Ice-Blue World before studying Chinese literature at university—a career author ever since. The "Our Seven Halls and Eight Departments" series—recently published in People's Literature and compiled into the anthology *Scorpio* (Shanghai Literature & Art Publishing House, 2018)—includes novellas like *Red Wine*, *Ambiguity*, *Lightbulb*, *Vacant Seat*, *Scorpio*, and *Three-Year Itch*. These works dissect the bureaucratic grind and middle-aged indignities with surgical precision, laying bare lives torn between professional servility and stubborn self-respect. The choice of subject stems, as the author admits, from having no other life to draw upon. "I've always dreaded reading peers' fiction," he confesses. "My classmates and I joke that after all my reading, only one theme emerges as both writable and masterable: despair. My peers had long staked their claims—harbors occupied, markets monopolized, territories carved up. Every literary peak flutters with righteous banners, swarming with Wu Song-esque heroes. Yet when I turned, I spotted one desolate outpost: my Seven Halls and Eight Departments." For "my friends exist outside literature—from department heads to clock-watching clerks, scattered across bureaucratic labyrinths. This is my elemental reality."①

These stories delve into bureaucratic spheres, chronicling civil servants' revolutionary posturing and romantic entanglements. Though the author portrays them as middle-aged realpolitik virtuosos groveling before systemic demands, their raw vulnerability exposes petty functionaries cornered by life—compromising, always compromising. The protagonists—invariably divorced, childless, mid-career men—juggle promotion anxieties and remarriage dilemmas. In the face of worldly calculations, Jian Fangping in Red Wine responds to Liu Jingli's ambiguous advances with unshaken confidence: "After all, I'm a deputy division-level cadre—what are you, Liu Jingli? A

① Nan Feiyan: "*My Seven Halls and Eight Departments*", http://www.360doc.cn/article/31642712_591309323.html

thirty-year-old woman putting on airs?" The process of indulging in this ambiguity is likened by him to "a first-time visitor to a buffet restaurant, suddenly confronted with an array of dishes to freely choose from—who would simply load their plate with a few slices of bread and call it a meal?" "A thirty-year-old woman—without career success, burdened by life experience, and lacking striking looks—her eagerness to marry him is understandable. But such desperation is unbecoming; it violates the unspoken rules of ambiguity, and a game that breaks its own rules cannot sustain itself." Similarly, in Ambiguity, Nie Yuchuan also evaluates his ambiguous relationships through the lens of bureaucratic rank.

Now, a Lin Daiyu-like figure has fallen from the sky—close friends with Director Zhong, once pursued him, and newly divorced. With all internal conditions met and external factors favorable, as long as he plays his cards right, why worry about Lao Sun snatching the deputy director position? Why fear missing the last bus of this major promotion round? Even if no promotions occur and the deputy director post remains vacant, he's only thirty-six this year. Trading time for space, accumulating small wins into major victories—he could simply outlast Lao Sun until retirement. For truly remarkable figures, one need only look to the present. Of course, this was all contingent—like a train with its schedule fixed, needing only to stay on track to eventually reach its destination—so long as it didn't derail. Now that his wife had drifted beyond reach, the very foundation for derailment no longer existed. As for playing with ambiguity—it could never be equated with derailment. Not only were they incomparable, but such dalliances might even yield unexpected rewards.

Light Bulb portrays the rare upright character Mu Shanbei—a man of unyielding integrity. While reviewing professorship materials, "he unceremoniously pulled out the Party secretary's wife's application, declaring her thesis fraudulent." When the leadership dismissed his objections and stamped "Preliminary Approval" anyway, Mu stormed into the office with her thesis demanding justification. Met with silence, he retreated to his dorm and penned a real-name whistle-blowing letter addressed directly to the Department's Senior Reviewing Committee. "This single incident made him notorious, shocking the entire department." Yet for years afterward, he was plagued by misfortune—passed over for promotions, labeled a "jinx," met with disdain and cold shoulders wherever he went. It wasn't until his transfer to the Ninth Division that his own growing desperation forced a change in attitude. Later, through his father-in-law's meticulous maneuvering, he was finally promoted to section chief. After muddling through over twenty years in the system, he finally realized that pursuing an official career didn't preclude being a shady, dim-witted yes-man. For him—"past forty now, with a son who's making him proud, a capable wife, and finally, a promotion of his own. If only his wife would fry him some spicy kidneys in the evening and his father-in-law would crack open a bottle of Erguotou, life would be just about perfect." Unlike the slick, worldly cynicism of other novels, *The Lightbulb* portrays an obstinately upright man struggling to fit in as a civil servant—one who refuses to falsify, flatter, compromise, or chase personal gain. He is a good man, yet perpetually sidelined, his life stifled by quiet indignities. As readers, we revel in Mu Shanbei's unapologetic adherence to his principles, especially in the cathartic episode where he storms the Fourth Audit Division. He had thoroughly humiliated Old Qi, leaving him no way out, then reduced Deputy Director Gao to speechless, crimson-faced fury. With a final nod to the onlookers, he strode away—"cutting through the crowd with an air of majestic dignity."* Yet this performance perfectly served the schemes of Xiao Xiao, the shrewd chief of the Ninth Division—orchestrating a tale where Xiao appeared the selfless team player, while framing Deputy Director Gao as the troublemaker. And Mu Shanbei, unwittingly playing the role of the leader's hatchet man, had secured his own promotion in the process.

"*Vacancy*" revolves around the competition for a state-sponsored position in a public institution. Xiao Meng, an undergraduate graduate, secures a logistical support role due to his father's nominal leadership position at the design institute—yet he continues striving for a fully-fledged *bianzhi* (state-approved staffing quota). Meanwhile, postgraduate Xiao Yan and her father are also locked in a covert battle for this very same position. Under Lao Meng's maneuvering, Xiao Yan initially found herself at a disadvantage. Despite her father being a section-level cadre, he resorted to drastic measures—leveraging his authority to insist on an audit, ultimately securing the coveted bianzhi position for his daughter. Meanwhile, Xiao Meng blackmailed Xiao Yan into a physical relationship. Their romantic history adds another layer of complexity: the two were once college sweethearts, but were forced to break up due to Xiao Meng's parents' disapproval. Years later, when they meet again, Xiao Meng remains a janitorial logistics worker, while Mei Ru has risen through the corporate ranks with remarkable success. The inequality in their status paradoxically rekindles their old flame. The true irony lies in Xiao Meng's awareness—he knows Mei Ru secured her position by submitting to their superior, with whom she continues the arrangement, yet he marries her regardless. For a man who has endured years of waiting for that elusive bianzhi, tormented by its absence, he has long since learned that dignity holds little weight against the harsh realities of survival.

The Xiao Meng of today was no longer the Xiao Meng of the past. He constantly reminded himself: all he wanted was a wife—a marriage—not some principled breakup over his girlfriend's infidelity. After all, her betrayal stemmed from the most basic survival instinct. Breaking up would be easy—a momentary satisfaction, but in the end, he'd gain nothing. How utterly pathetic. After all these years at the research institute, if he couldn't even calculate this simple equation, then his time there would have been truly wasted.

This story leaves readers with a profound sense of tragedy. The once-idealistic young man—"starting with his pursuit of that vacant bianzhi, had, over the years, buried his ideals, dignity, and moral bottom line one by one."*

The same holds true for Xiao Yan: a music graduate student who sold herself out for that very position, offering her body to Xiao Meng. Mei Ru's story is no different. It forces us to confront the brutal reality of human alienation—how easily humanity crumbles before the onslaught of profit and temptation.

These bureaucrats and functionaries have fought their entire lives over positions, only to gain clarity on the brink of retirement. In Scorpio, the author channels Old Feng's lament: "You're still middle-aged, kid, but I'm pushing sixty. At this stage, if you've got your health, a modest nest egg, obedient kids, a wife who hasn't left, and a career that's at least respectable—that's enough. As for promotions and riches? They don't add much, nor does their absence take much away. When you really think about it, it's all just a fucking charade." Outsiders may remain detached, but for those trapped within the system, the sheer calculation they must employ and the indignities they endure are truly distressing—revealing both the terrifying nature of humanity under modern competitive mechanisms and the brutal difficulty of mere survival.

3. The Life Struggles of Youth

Chen Hongwei's *The Secret of the Triangle* explores the hidden tensions within an urban family across three generations—two interlocking triangles that uphold a seemingly stable structure. The grandfather, suspecting his grandson is not biologically his son's, demands a paternity test. Only then does the grandmother reveal the long-buried truth: their son was never the husband's biological child to begin with. Meanwhile, the daughter-in-law had indeed been unfaithful. To preserve marital harmony, she and her lover conspired to forge a fake paternity test. Thus, each family member lives in silent complicity, yet all still crave the solace of love and warmth.

Zhou Yichen started from the very bottom of the bureaucratic ladder—a low-level clerk who honed his skills through a decade of meticulous work, weathering countless upheavals and setbacks. A man without his tenacity would have surely given up long ago. Many of his peers, meanwhile, had taken up calligraphy, photography, or outdoor hobbies like cycling and mountain climbing. They dodged responsibilities at every turn, having seemingly seen through the futility of bureaucratic struggle, now reclaiming their passion for life beyond the office. Yet he remains undeterred, vigorously performing his duties as a deputy section chief (with the perks of a full section chief)—his lifelong goal being to shed those parentheses and rise to the actual position, finally tasting the power of being the man in charge.

Liu Lili often mocks him for blurring the line between desire and ambition, thus disguising his grubby cravings as lofty ideals.[①]

In contrast, his son Zhou Yichen is a simpler man—passionate about his work, driven by ideals. Kindhearted and principled, even when suspecting the paternity test's validity, he insists: "I won't let this anger me. No matter

---

① Chen Hongwei. *The Secret of the Triangle*. Fiction Monthly (Original Edition), no. 3, 2016.

what, I'll keep loving my son as always. But after last night's reflection, I've decided to take Hanghang for another test." In this context, the wife's rekindled first love and subsequent disorientation lay bare the unsettling uncertainties of modern romantic games. "Perhaps on some sun-drenched afternoon, he would invite her to the countryside, tracing the creek upstream in search of waterfalls. He led her down secluded paths unknown even to seasoned hikers, where they discovered wild peach trees heavy with autumn fruit. Or he'd take her to that newly opened Sichuan hotpot joint on Shenbei Road, watching bianlian face-changing performances between mouthfuls of spicy broth. She knew he was trying—trying to show her novel wonders. To parade the world's glitter before her eyes, then pull her onto a carousel." Romance and impermanence intertwine, breeding life's unsettling uncertainties. Thus, they seek a stable stage to begin their marital life—only to be entangled in generational sagas of origin.

In *So Distant the Horizon*, a former couple chooses divergent paths: one settles in the small town of Xinyang, while the other ventures to Guangzhou to conquer the world—their stories diverging through fate and psyche.

Yang Yi admired Yunhan for seemingly always carrying dreams within her—though she never clearly articulated what those dreams were. Yet they seemed to linger somewhere beyond, and she was forever chasing them. As for Yang Yi, living in the small city of Xinyang, if he had any dream at all, it was simply to live idly: parents in good health, a harmonious family, a happy child, and a stable job—these formed the quiet reality of his life, yet also the deepest wish of his heart. Not long after, Yang Yi seized an opportunity: he purchased a farmer's house near Nanwan Lake. The farmer had left for the city, settling into urban life. Nestled against the hillside by the lakeshore, the property boasted a two-story, three-room home, a private well, and a spacious courtyard. Trees draped its front and back, vines clambering up the walls—all for just 250,000 yuan. Yang Yi enlisted a painter friend to design a renovation that embraced the local materials, transforming them through resourceful adaptation. The interior was furnished entirely with vintage solid-wood pieces, polished to a spotless gleam. At the center of the main hall hung his painter friend's reproduction of the classical landscape Travelers Among Mountains and Streams, flanked by a couplet in clerical script: "A sudden flash of inspiration—poetry worthy of wine; A surge of bold passion—a sword fit to gift a friend." Below, a blue-and-white Guanyin vase stood on the desk, alongside leisurely reads like *Eight Treatises on Nurturing Life* and *Lakeside Notes*...

What was meant to be a reclusive life, indifferent to worldly strife, became, for the weary city-weary Shaohan, an object of deep envy. "You know what? In big cities now, food safety is a serious issue. You were so visionary! I want to return to my hometown too—till a plot of land, grow my own vegetables, eat what I sow, with nothing but blue skies and white clouds overhead...to live a life straight out of pastoral poetry." "Yang Yi, I used to think life in a small city was insufferably dull—but now I see how wrong I was.

Though I lived in a metropolis, I'd turned my existence into ruins..." Yet when she quit her big-city job and returned to Xinyang to adopt a child, pouring all her savings into rescuing a poor girl, she was met with nothing but deception. The cruelty of poverty struck her with brutal unexpectedness. Yang Yi lived his idle, unhurried life in that small town, while Shaohan—yearning to retreat from the turbulent tides of the metropolis—found there was, in fact, nowhere left to retreat to.

The novella *On Filmmaking* follows a young man's journey into cinema—only to reveal a director whose grasp of market forces and social currents leads him to a ruthless axiom: "'Never make films with artistic ideals—that kind of goodwill will get you trampled like donkey offal,' he told me. 'In this era, ideals are the cheapest currency. Filmmaking is like seducing women: the moment you take it seriously, you lose.' Seeing my confusion, he clenched his fist: 'Movies are playthings—to indulge the brain-dead masses.'" The entire filmmaking process descends into farce, riddled with backdoor dealings and societal ills—only the investor clings to artistic ideals, while everyone else chases profit. The novella even skewers "those film critics who, after one viewing, deliver grandiose critiques as if ruling an empire. They fail to grasp that cinema is mass entertainment, not avant-garde elitist art. What a tragedy—watching films with some lofty spiritual motive."[①] The film deconstructs the very process of filmmaking—where money and desire

① Chen Hongwei. *On Filmmaking*. Feitian (Skyward), no. 5, 2016.

dictate every move. It lays bare the story of actresses confronting the industry's unspoken rules, choosing self-abandonment in the face of exploitation. The investor, though driven by artistic ideals, lacks cinematic craft; meanwhile, the operators, well-versed in societal games, treat the project as a vehicle for profit. The young, already steeped in worldly cunning, navigate this speculative landscape with practiced ease.

The short story *Sunrise Viewing* captures a young couple's overwhelming sense of helplessness against life's pressures. Liu Xiaojuan and her husband Li Dongdong, college sweethearts, both stayed in Shencheng after graduation. Yet Xiaojuan harbors one simple wish: to take her family to see the sunrise at Rooster Mountain. Li Dongdong scoffed: "Rooster Mountain isn't San Francisco—what kind of wish is that? Hardly worth mentioning." Though merely 50 kilometers from the city, the family never quite made the trip. Yet ironically, Dongdong had accompanied his boss, friends, relatives, and classmates there—only for this seemingly trivial wish to remain perpetually unfulfilled for his own family. Amid the mounting pressures—mortgage payments, his wife's layoff, his mother's illness—the wish faded into oblivion. Then, when their daughter needed to write an essay about watching a sunrise, the family was stirred into action—only to face soaring park fees due to foreign investment: 400+ yuan for a night's lodging, tickets jacked up from 30 to 80 yuan, turning the plan into another round of "we'll do it later." And the wife, ground down by life, shed every last trace of poetry in her soul.

Liu Xiaojuan's newsstand ballooned into a multi-service hub: collecting utility bills, charging e-bikes, selling daily necessities, and even brokering motorcycle helmets. She toiled from dawn to dusk, drowning in petty chores and scattered feathers—yet beneath it all, life remained a crude, repetitive simplicity, its rhythm so rigid it bordered on the mechanical. The elderly customers would fumble through last month's utility receipts, squinting at the fine print. Liu Xiaojuan waited patiently—when their eyes failed them, she'd even take the slips, decipher the details, and explain until their worries eased. Once, she'd been proud of her glossy black hair, a standout feature at the factory. Now, it hung dull and brittle, exuding an air of exhaustion. Without realizing it, she had "barged" her way into becoming the epitome of a hardened, streetwise woman.

Then came the day when they finally set out—determined to visit Rooster Mountain, stay overnight, and at last witness the sunrise. Their daughter Yingying leapt with excitement, vowing to write a six-hundred-word essay about the experience. Their high-spirited trip collapsed when they discovered Rooster Mountain no longer offered sunrise views—the path to Dawn-Crowing Peak was blocked by a stone wall, officially because "the new city mayor, born in the Year of the Rooster, couldn't bear hordes trampling the rooster's head—it might hinder his promotion…" The family stood stunned, gaping wordlessly at the distant peak. Through this trivial wish for a sunrise, the story lays bare the quiet tragedies of ordinary lives—the helplessness, the bitterness, the cruel absurdity of it all.

Chen Hongwei's fiction excavates profound resonance from the mundane—stories like *Group Photo* and *So Distant the Horizon* trace how two college friends, once mutually attracted, diverge: one chasing metropolitan dreams, the other rooted in a small town. Their shifting mindsets and fortunes lay bare life's inexhaustible melancholy. *Sunrise Viewing* carries the same essence as *A Wilderness of Feathers*—young adults entering society, crushed under the weight of survival: parents and children, mortgages and cars, social obligations—all weaving an inescapable net, leaving them powerless and trapped. Meanwhile, *The Secret of the Triangle* explores the precarious balance of modern families and the multifaceted nature of love and marriage. *On Filmmaking* lays bare the clash between idealism and worldly cynicism—and the latter's ruthless dominance. These stories, steeped in the raw vitality of everyday life and the divergent choices of youth, unfold a kaleidoscope of urban struggles.

4. Confronting Urban Aging Issues

Zhou Daxin's *The Slow Darkening* (published by People's Literature Publishing House, January 2018) stands as China's first full-length novel to confront the realities of an aging society—a poignant exploration of time's erosion on the individual and the city itself. Since 2015, China has entered a period of rapid population aging, with projections indicating that by 2035, the elderly will comprise 20% of the population. As aging escalates into a critical social issue, this novel serves as both a warning and a testament to literature's dual role—aesthetic and social—in confronting demographic upheaval.

For decades, our society has worshipped youth with near-religious fervor. Liang Qichao's "*Youthful China*" famously declared: "The old are like monks, the young like knights-errant"; "The old resemble opium smoke, the young, brandy." "When youth are strong, the nation is strong; when youth progress, the nation progresses." This rhetoric has since dominated cultural narratives—from *Song of Youth* to *The Younger Generation* and *Long Live Youth*—all hymns to the cult of youth. Even today, screens are monopolized by "fresh-faced male idols" and "beautiful maidens", while literary depictions of the elderly remain confined to archetypes: the authoritative patriarch (e.g., clan elders) or the mystic sage (like the Old Master in *Extremely Flower*). They exist as symbols, not flesh-and-blood humans.

This novel truly portrays the elderly as human—tracking its protagonist from age 73 to 86, from defiant denial to organ failure, mapping his psychological journey, struggles, and emotions with unprecedented depth, thus enriching contemporary literature's gallery of characters. A hardened former judge, he would still seethe when offered a seat on the bus in his seventies, waging a relentless war against decline through desperate acts of self-preservation. He visited matchmaking agencies, yearning for love and marriage. When he met a compatible woman, he poured effort into the relationship—only to fail due to his declining health and her pragmatic calculations. In his quest to defy aging, he dabbled in bizarre remedies: clapping exercises, guiling turtle-longevity qigong, consuming "Thousand-Year Elixir" ointments, etc. Naturally, his journey was riddled with scams—a stark reflection of societal exploitation targeting the vulnerable. Yet by confronting these harsh realities head-on, the novel forces public reckoning, showcasing the author's unflinching courage and narrative innovation.

Think carefully: virtually every elderly person around us has been targeted—bombarded with aggressive marketing, brainwashing sales tactics pushing dubious "health supplements" and miracle elixirs. The novel's scenes strike a visceral chord because this is the unvarnished truth—the lived reality of elders among us. In their battle against aging and their desperate grasp for longevity, they've tried everything—exhausted every effort. Yet faced with a society of grotesque absurdities, after emotional and financial betrayals, where can the elderly turn? The author constructs a utopian retreat—an unpolluted "longevity village" of pristine simplicity. Yet as urbanites, we all know such a life is irrecoverable. Thus, aging remains an intractable social crisis, with no pristine escape.

Moreover, the novel's structure itself is strikingly unconventional. It opens with a bombardment of cutting-edge technologies: companion robots, Lingqi Longevity Pills, virtual reality age-reversal experiences—a parade of ostensibly utopian futures. Yet behind this facade lies the naked truth of existence: human greed and selfishness, love's betrayals and abandonments, the inexorable decay of organs and nature's unforgiving laws—elderly souls left to wander empty houses and boundless solitude. Technology and emotion thus form a dialectical tension. In this interim period—before science can effectively combat aging and death—how should humanity cope? Can technological progress and emotional resilience coexist symbiotically? Here lies profound ground for reflection.

This is a work that captures the raw, unvarnished emotions of human bonds: a father's love for his daughter, manifesting as relentless disdain for her husband; a daughter's love for her spouse, driving her to abortion, exile, depression—even death; a caregiver's love for her partner, laboring to fund his university and graduate studies. When these individuals depart, an unlikely family emerges—a retired judge, his caregiver, and a child. To secure the child's urban hukou, the two enter a marriage of convenience, only to develop a profound father-daughter bond over years of shared struggle. Then, as the judge succumbs to advanced dementia, nearing death—long past medical salvation, at the point where most would abandon hope—the caregiver transcends her role, summoning a mother's love, attempting to rouse him through the most primal human connections.

Since the dawn of modernity, loneliness and desire have become humanity's eternal burdens. Life, stripped of tranquility and warmth, loses the capacity for love. Our existence is shackled by real estate mania and material obsession—literature now overrun by scheming opportunists and conspirators, from palace intrigues to corporate dramas and domestic sagas. Genuine emotion has been exiled to the margins. Such works may sharpen our survival skills, yet they fail to stir the soul—only deepening the world's cruelty, freezing hearts further. But the power of emotion remains eternal, the very essence of being human. Even in the most irreverent *A Chinese Odyssey*, the rogue Zhizunbao preserves a single tear of love within. And in the spectacle-driven *Avengers: Infinity War*, Thanos—capable of annihilating galaxies—still sheds a tender tear for his adopted daughter. Yet today, we've grown dangerously dismissive of emotion, obsessively fixated on materiality. As Lukács' theory of reification warns: humanity has become enslaved to objects, and relationships between people now mirror transactions between commodities. This is our stark reality. If success and happiness are measured solely in material terms, we lose the authenticity of life itself. That's why this novel's emotional power strikes with such force—it defies the tyranny of things.

Since his literary debut in 1979, Zhou Daxin has crafted a remarkable oeuvre over four decades—works like *Han Jia' Daughter*, *The Twentieth Curtain*, *Lakeside Scenery*, *Early Warning*, and *When the Music Ends*. Though varying in historical settings, character archetypes, and social critiques, his novels share an unwavering engagement with contemporary currents, each a mirror held up to its time. Take *Lakeside Scenery*—it captures a mountain village's upheavals under market economy forces, while *When the Music Ends* confronts the moral labyrinth of anti-corruption. As Zhou's career progressed, avoiding repetition of others' work was challenging enough—but surpassing his own precedents demanded even more. Thus, his later works became definitive syntheses, distilling and elevating all that came before. Zhou Daxin defies this pattern—each work reinvents perspective, setting, character, and theme, a testament to his uncompromising literary rigor. *Slowly the Darkness Falls* confronts aging society's crises, not merely exposing social ills but relentlessly probing solutions.

The narrative unfolds in an urban park—seven dusks weave together this novel's tapestry. Slowly the darkness falls, its chill and warmth etched in silence. Classical poetry long captured twilight's duality—the lingering ache of "The setting sun flares sublime, yet twilight looms" or the desolate pang of "No bitterness compares to dusk's descent." Zhou's novel unlocks twilight through myriad lenses, immersing us in the raw realities of those who inhabit its fading light.

Chapter 8
How Cities Become a State of Mind

1. What Is Urban Consciousness

What exactly is urban consciousness? Why do so many writers, even after decades in the city, still insist "I am a peasant at heart"? Why does the city's identity remain so elusive—is it merely a labyrinth of skyscrapers isolating rootless individuals, or does it manifest distinct urban temperaments? Conventional literary approaches have often relied on excavating urban histories, constructing a sense of belonging through collective memory. Yet we must not overlook urban modernity—the forces shaping city-dwellers' lived realities today, and how these dynamics construct urban identity. Many writers weave historical memory with the restlessness of the contemporary—capturing neon-lit novelties and fleeting scenes—interrogating both past and present to reveal the city's fractured visage and the pathologies of our time.

Professor Chen Xiaoming, in his essay "*Urban Literature: Detours and Dilemmas*," offers a seminal definition: "So-called urban literature is work that depicts city life while embodying a distinct urban consciousness." But what constitutes "urban consciousness"? "It means the narrator or characters are perpetually aware of the city's presence—how their existential conditions and ways of life are entangled with urbanity. They actively interrogate their state of being within the city. In most cases, this mirrors modern individual self-awareness, which could even be distilled as Romantic, Modernist, or Postmodernist consciousness..." Urban literature in the post-Reform era arguably only reconnected with the "minor tradition" of modern metropolitan writing in the 1990s—through works by the "New Generation" and "Post-70s" authors. Yet their urban narratives often skew toward the superficial and decorative. As self-proclaimed urbanites, did these writers truly internalize the city's spirit in their craft? Indeed, urban literature must be rooted in an urban ethos—one that transcends the glittering decadence of high society to embrace the raw, unspoken struggles of the marginalized."①

Urban culture manifests in the collective psyche, values, beliefs, and behavioral norms of city-dwellers—this is urban consciousness. By definition, urban consciousness exists in dialectical opposition to rural consciousness. On one hand, the city assaults its inhabitants with dense crowds, frenetic rhythms, and sensory overload—forcing people to "learn urban adaptation" through rigid time-space organization and reinvented survival strategies. Thus emerges a cluster of values and beliefs—utilitarian, scientific, aggressively "progressive." Yet simultaneously, sheer population density, cutthroat competition, and commodity fetishism spawn urban maladaptation: temporal-spatial anxiety, behavioral aberrations, money sickness, existential void, and the alienation of dehumanization—all hallmarks of the city's pathological psyche.②

For Henan, the interplay between cultural heritage and urban modernity

---

① Liu Bo et al. "*The Spiritual Foundation and Realistic Dilemmas of Urban Literature*" [J]. Yangtze River Literary Review, no. 3, 2018.

② Xu Jianyi. "Urban Culture and Urban Literature: The Cultural Characteristics and Formation of Contemporary Urban Fiction" [J]. Literary Review, no. 5, 1987.

defines its cities' unique character. The longstanding slogan "Henan, Our Ancestral Home" proclaims the province as the root of Chinese civilization—evidenced by sites like Laozi's Lecture Platform, Du Fu's Hometown, and Li Shangyin Park. Yet as modernity advances, integrating tradition with contemporary life poses fresh challenges. This is why Henan's eight-minute promotional video, showcased by the Ministry of Foreign Affairs, brims with cultural symbolism—from ancient capitals like Zhengzhou (Xia-Shang), Luoyang (13 dynasties), Kaifeng (8 dynasties), and Anyang (7 dynasties) as cradles of Chinese civilization, to cultural icons such as the Longmen Grottoes, Yin Ruins, Shaolin Temple, and Taiji Zen, alongside modern landmarks including the "Golden Corn" Tower and Aviation Port, weaving together antiquity and futurism. By seamlessly blending tradition with contemporary flair, and gravitas with urban vitality, it stands as a paradigm of masterful city branding. In literary works, the quest for urban identity is far more subtle and introspective than its overt, visual representations. Yet writers persistently mine these depths—probing their characters' lived environments, excavating narrative spaces where stories germinate, and sifting through the turbulent interplay of tradition and modernity that defines contemporary lives.

2. Rustic Meets Cosmopolitan in *The Plain Climber*

Li Peifu's latest work, *The Plain Climber*, stands out as his most cosmopolitan novel to date, interwoven with modern elements and the author's evolving perspectives. The protagonist, though of rural origins, ascends to urban life through the national college entrance exam, eventually marrying the beautiful daughter of a professor. His journey culminates in earning a doctorate at Columbia University in the U.S.—a modern intellectual baptized in Western learning, yet forever marked by his earthy roots. Yet years of hamburgers never altered his palate, nor did Westernized living transform his soul—outwardly, he remained a farmer at heart. Even as a prestigious vice-chancellor, he was "more peasant than any peasant, a wizened little old man", appearing utterly mismatched with his elegant, refined wife in the eyes of their students. Ultimately, this marriage collapsed under the weight of its contradictions. Later, as a high-ranking vice governor, his sole requirement for remarriage was an uneducated rural woman—someone to tend to his aging father. A wheat scientist bound to the soil by visceral ties, his choices seemed understandable. Yet what defies comprehension is this: could decades of urban ascent truly leave his habits and thought patterns fossilized?

In his first marriage, the "Five Commandments" imposed on his ex-wife included: no smoking indoors, cultivating proper hygiene, maintaining a presentable appearance, changing into clean clothes before going out and slippers upon entering, and mandatory tooth-brushing, face-washing, hand-scrubbing, and foot-cleaning before bed. Such constraints suffocated him. When remarrying, he spurned college graduates, demanding instead a "practical" woman—one who could care for others, share meals with his father, even if uneducated. Thus came Xu Ercai, a peasant girl turned live-in maid, until her coarseness and threats became unbearable, driving him to indirect murder and his own downfall—a marital tragedy precipitating existential ruin. If his first marriage collapsed under the strain of incompatibility—a professor's daughter wed to a farmer's son—the second marriage, though seemingly matched in class, spiraled into greater tragedy through unbridgeable spiritual divides. The novel probes a central paradox: how seemingly charmed lives unravel, and how one navigates the chasm between material success and spiritual desolation.

Through the character of Inspector Helian Dongshan, the author interrogates generational divides. A decorated officer yet estranged from his son, he views the boy's gaming obsession and defiance as the epitome of failure—a bitter irony for a man who upholds order professionally yet cannot govern his own household. Yet this "failure" of a son earned cash selling gaming gear in college, and by graduation commanded annual salaries of 300,000 to 500,000 yuan—six to ten times his father's lifelong "revolutionary work" income of 50,000 yuan. The absurd climax? The inspector demands his son quit this "unserious" job for traditional employment. When a "post-90s" fan of his son's lashed out at him, the rebuke—unexpectedly—cracked open a moment of self-reckoning.

On a Beijing business trip, his son took him to a Russian restaurant—"This is wholly a young people's universe," he observed. "Amid melancholic Russian melodies, clinking wine glasses and scraping cutlery on steak, men lean into women's shoulders, women nestle in men's arms—laughter, kisses, whispers, and toasts swirling in an unbroken stream.""Suddenly, the music shifted—in a flash, a marching tempo erupted. A squad (four men) of towering Russians in vintage Red Army uniforms materialized, parading between tables, belting "Katyusha" in thunderous unison!"

In this overwhelming atmosphere, Helian Dongshan felt not only lightheaded but also visually disoriented—a visceral disconnection between memory and reality. Russian songs had been the anthems of Helian Dongshan's youth—romantic ideals that once nourished his soul like unattainable lovers. To Helian Dongshan, those Red Army uniforms—their epaulets and insignia—embodied an era forged in blood and sacrifice. Regardless of historical judgment, they deserved a fundamental reverence as relics of their time. Yet here, they were reduced to mere dinner theater—seasoning for steak and vodka.①

To the red-haired, hoop-earringed "post-90s" generation, Helian Dongshan was just a fossil—a provincial relic. And deep down, he knew: "This era no longer belongs to you."

The chasm between father and son transcends mere generational gaps—it mirrors how rapidly shifting realities reshape human psyches. A fractured society breeds fractured selves. "From ancient records until the 1990s, China

① Li Peifu. *The Plain Climber* [M]. Guangzhou: Flower City Press, 2014, p.233.

remained fundamentally an agrarian civilization, riddled with stark regional divides in dialect and culture."[①] During the Mao era, minimal social mobility and enforced ideological conformity created a monolithic cultural landscape. With Deng Xiaoping's reforms deepening, China underwent a seismic shift—from an agrarian society to an urbanized one, while opening windows to the globalized world. The dissolution of hyper-stable social structures, compounded by relentless change and cultural influx, has spawned a kaleidoscopic reality—where fractures and disparities multiply.

According to sociological studies: "China's youth today, born under the post-reform one-child policy, were lavished with undivided familial devotion—yet now face the brutal disparities and competition of a market economy. Global consumer culture offers material abundance, but coexisting value systems spawn existential bewilderment and paralyzing choice...These forces forge a generational signature—a distinct social experience and collective identity that sets them apart from their parents not just in age, but in consciousness, values, and life trajectories. Their parents, products of Mao-era planned economies, were steeped in orthodox collectivism and traditional familial ethos, only to endure the convulsions of transition—wrenching reforms in education, employment, welfare, domesticity, and core values. Thus, the 'generation gap' between them transcends biology—it's a palimpsest of familial bonds, historical epochs, and institutional upheavals. These forces

① (US) Ezra F. Vogel, *Deng Xiaoping and the Transformation of China*, SDX Joint Publishing Company, 2013, p. 650.

intersect dynamically, breeding fractures in social conditions and cultural logic, and laying the groundwork for pervasive intergenerational strife."[1]

Thus, Li Peifu's literary "plains" evolve—accommodating both the staunch '50s generation with their rigid codes of honor, idealism, and even their dichotomous view of "proper" versus "improper" work, and the idiosyncratic post-80s/90s cohorts who declare "My youth, my rules!"—uncompromising in their pursuit of selfhood. Beneath its fragmented surface, this novel unveils the city's multidimensional reality—where generational worldviews collide, urban/rural upbringings dictate cognitive divides, and lifestyles fracture along class lines. The author sutures rural youth to Ivy League PhDs, interweaves bureaucrats with entrepreneurs, constructing a polyphonic urban tapestry. This urban landscape hybridizes tradition and modernity—where time-honored Heji Noodle shops coexist with neon-lit clubs, where the century-old Dehua Bathhouse of Kaifeng—with its masterful artisans—exists alongside neon-lit massage parlors staffed by migrant women. The city is a Frankenstein of rusticity and cosmopolitanism, its inhabitants both shaping and being reshaped by the streets they walk.

---

① Wu Xiaoying. "Intergenerational Conflict and the Evolution of Youth Discourse" [J]. Youth Studies, no. 8, 2006.

3. Weight and Weightlessness in *The Pearl Journal*

The Pearl Journal (published by Writers Publishing House in 2017) is Qiao Ye's magical realist novel, blending the mundane with the fantastical. Qiao Ye's earlier works confront reality unflinchingly: *I Truly Love You* traces the struggles of migrant sisters, *Demolition Diary* exposes urbanization's chaos through documentary rawness, and *The Confession* excavates the trauma of the "Cultural Revolution" to reveal humanity's darkest folds. Her new work, *The Pearl Journal*, introduces an ageless woman—a millennia-old existence sustained by a single mystical pearl.

In the year 755, a dying Persian merchant—grateful to his landlord couple—bestowed their daughter with an immortality-granting pearl. Thus, "the girl lived on...and on, from the Tang Dynasty to the present, an undying relic outlasting even the silk-wrapped case, its inscribed poem long dust—only these carved verses remained in her mind: The pearl's strange fragrance lingers eternal / Through storm and snow its glow prevails / Break its bond, longevity crumbles / Spit it out, mortality reclaims."① Bound by that parchment's decree and shielded by the pearl's power, she endured a millennium—until this fantastical premise unfurled into an achingly human love story.

In recent years, the Tang pearl found its way to Zhengzhou—becoming

① Qiao Ye. *The Pearl Journal* [M]. Beijing: Writers Publishing House, 2017, pp. 4-5.

an unwitting witness to the city's metamorphosis.

A decade ago, this villa district in southeastern Zhengzhou debuted with grand promises of "exclusivity and prestige," its opening price a mere 2,000 yuan per square meter. Today, that figure has skyrocketed to nearly 20,000. Back then, passing by occasionally, I could still glimpse ruddy brick walls draped in green construction nets—and catch the grassy scent of cornfields wafting from nearby. Now, encircled by skyscrapers, one would need to trek ten li to glimpse open fields.

Tempered by millennia of witness, the pearl carries a weary wisdom: "Under the sun, nothing is truly new." From Tang to Song, Yuan to Ming, Qing to Republic—even now—only the costumes change. Human dramas replay with altered sets and scripts, but the core remains unchanged across dynasties and republics. If the world's surface races like meteors chasing the moon, human nature spins in place—wearing the ground into an ever-deepening rut. Yet this very lucidity, born of love's lethal terror, makes her sever each romance, retreating into solitude—until her love for Jinze shatters all restraint. Love dissolves history, erases inherited burdens, lifts the pearl's ancient shadows—until at last, unshackled from all weight, they find happiness.

This seemingly straightforward tale—an immortal woman's love for a mortal man, overcoming all odds—belies layered complexities. It straddles the weight of history (Tang-era lore, Henan cuisine's intricate heritage) and the lightness of modernity (a love-and-conspiracy thriller triggered by a mere USB drive). Ultimately, love's pleasure principle triumphs—over history's shadows and society's vulgar pragmatism—epitomizing modernity's urban ethos. Freud theorized that the ego emerges from the id, serving as a mediator between the individual and society. It embodies the moral and rational dictates of the superego—the social conscience. In his famous metaphor, the id is a "galloping wild horse," while the ego acts as its "rider," striving to steer primal urges with reason.[①] Within this psychic structure, the id operates on the pleasure principle (immediate instinctual gratification), while the ego adheres to the reality principle (social norms and moral conscience). The reality principle suppresses or postpones the id's demands, creating civilization's inherent repression of primal drives. Freud argued that societal "progress" manifests as technology's domination over life and reason's conquest of humanity—a pyrrhic victory costing profound losses. His psychoanalytic lens exposed modernity's central conflict: the irreconcilable clash between the pleasure principle and reality principle.

In *The Pearl Journal*, all contradictions dissolve—even the pearl's millennia-old covenant with its bearer vanishes. Here, the reality principle harmonizes with the pleasure principle, merging history with the present, while elevating the mundane to poetic focus. Gone are grand narratives and existential missions—the focus narrows to the daily rhythms of two lovers bound

① Schultz, Duane P. *A History of Modern Psychology* [M]. Translated by Shen Decan et al. Beijing: People's Education Press, 1981, pp. 342-343.

by food. Through lavish depictions of Henan cuisine, the author forges a gastronomic metaphor: dishes become human, humans become dishes, their fusion embodying transcendent harmony.

The status of our Henan cuisine? It's the mother of all Chinese culinary traditions.

Unapologetically speaking, the entire evolution of Chinese gastronomy—from its embryonic origins to its golden age—unfolded in the Central Plains. Henan cuisine's roots are deeply imperial—as the heartland of four of China's Eight Ancient Capitals (excluding Zhengzhou's shorter reign), it boasts Anyang and Kaifeng as seven-dynasty capitals, while Luoyang served as the seat of power for nine dynasties across a staggering 1,500 years. Consider how effortlessly imperial dishes would have trickled down to the masses.

Henan cuisine achieves perfect equilibrium—sweet but not cloying, tart but not sharp, salty but never harsh, spicy yet restrained, delicate without blandness, fragrant without greasiness... Don't laugh. This is the zenith of culinary finesse. No distinct traits? Nonsense. Our essence lies in licorice's role in traditional medicine—harmonizing all flavors with perfect equipoise. Hence the gourmet's adage: Canton feasts, Sichuan dazzles, but balance reigns in the Central Plains.[①]

---

① Qiao Ye. *The Pearl Journal* [M]. Beijing: Writers Publishing House, 2017, pp. 123-125.

Henan's culinary culture permeates the entire narrative with striking vitality—echoing *The Book of Rites*: "Food and intimacy, these are humanity's primal desires." Through its gastronomic archaeology and alchemy of human-dish fusion, the narrative bridges ancient and modern urban ethos—transforming millennia of historical weight into the paradoxical lightness of contemporary repetition.

Epilogue: The Triumph of Cities and New Literary Horizons

In *Triumph of the City*, Edward Glaeser traces how "since Plato and Socrates debated in Athenian agoras, dense urban clusters have served as humanity's engines of innovation. Florence's cobblestones birthed the Renaissance; Birmingham's lanes ignited the Industrial Revolution. Today, London, Bangalore, and Tokyo thrive precisely because they generate ideas. Strolling these cities—whether along pebbled walkways, sprawling intersections, roundabouts, or freeways—one witnesses only the relentless march of human progress."① Yet the author also argues that urban development must fiercely safeguard its physical past.

This year marks the 40th anniversary of China's Reform and Opening-up—a milestone celebrated across literary circles. As we reflect on these dec-

① (US) Glaeser, Edward. *Triumph of the City* [M]. Trans. Liu Runquan. Shanghai: Shanghai Academy of Social Sciences Press, 2012, p. 1.

ades, urbanization's meteoric rise emerges as the defining narrative, inseparable from the epic saga of rural-to-urban migration etched in countless novels: from Lu Yao's *Life*, where Gao Jialin embodies the struggles of a liminal generation straddling rural and urban worlds, to Gao Xiaosheng's *Chen Huansheng Goes to the City* with its disorienting urban awakening, to Li Peifu's *City Lights* and its ruthless break with the past, and Zhang Yigong's *Distant Post Station* excavating buried metropolitan memories. Cities are ceaselessly narrated spaces—and as society evolves and writers' insights deepen, urban literary portraits grow increasingly layered. Jia Pingwa's *Happy* exposes the gritty realities of marginalized urban lives, while Yu He's essays probe the spiritual dimensions of city dwellers, collectively expanding the possibilities of urban literature.

Henan, though long a stronghold of rural narratives, has consistently made rural literature its dominant tradition—from Shi Tuo's modernist *Orchard City* in early contemporary literature to Li Zhun's *That Road is Forbidden* at the dawn of new China's literature, and onward to the "literary maps" of Yan Lianke and Liu Zhenyun (depicting the Balou Mountains and Yanjin County), Li Peifu's "Plains Trilogy", and Li Er's *Peaches on a Pomegranate Tree*—all rooted in the native soil that defines Henan's literary ethos. If the "Shanxi Literary Campaign" period used rural narratives to encapsulate a century of Chinese culture, Henan's roots in rural literature run even deeper—as the primary vessel of Yellow River civilization. Tracing the common threads among Henan writers through this literary lineage demands urgent scholarly attention. In these writers' works, the bond with the land emerges as the most enduring narrative. In contemporary literature alone, Yan Lianke's Balou Mountains and Liu Zhenyun's Yanjin County—through decades of creative output—have crystallized into canonical literary landscapes. Since first charting the Balou Mountains in the 1980s, Yan Lianke's oeuvre has remained deeply rooted in his homeland. Works like *Dreams of the Yaogou People*, *Years, Months, Days*, and *Chronicle of a Blood Merchant* excavate a mythic rural cosmos—where love for the land intertwines with existential toil, each page saturated with struggle. Liu Zhenyun stands as a uniquely significant figure—from *Ta Pu* (nostalgic recollections of youth) to the neo-realist grit of *A Wilderness of Feathers*, he maintained quiet dedication amid the 1990s market frenzies. His "Hometown Trilogy" (*Yellow Flowers of Home*, *Hometown Noodles and Flowers*, Hometown Legends) culminated in *Someone to Talk To*—a Mao Dun Prize winner hailed as China's One Hundred Years of Solitude—yet his gaze never wavered from the wisdom and resilience of rural China.

By contrast, Li Peifu—who has steadfastly written within Henan's borders—epitomizes regional literary dedication. His Mao Dun Prize-winning *The Book of Life* stands as a testament to decades of narrative mastery rooted in local soil. Since *The Sheep's Gate* in the 1990s, Li Peifu has been a pillar of Central Plains literature—his obsessive depictions of flora, soil, and Henan's entrenched power structures deliver visceral impact. Yet, despite its brilliance, this masterpiece never received its due acclaim.[1] With 2012's *The Book of Life*—hailed as the finale of his "Plains Trilogy" (following *The Sheep's Gate* and *City Lights*)—Li Peifu synthesized three decades of writing into a spiritual odyssey, simultaneously composing an elegy for the ages. The protagonist Wu Zhipeng—an orphan nourished by Wuliang Village's communal milk and rice—becomes a university teacher in the provincial capital after graduating. Yet, his rural upbringing remains an inescapable "heavy tail" (metaphor for lingering burden). No matter how his life changes, his hometown lingers like a shadow in his existence. To completely break free from the countryside and its shadow, he resigns from his public teaching position and plunges into private business. Yet, despite enduring countless hardships, he never finds inner peace—only then does he realize that his rural roots and himself have always shared the same lifeblood. For Li Peifu, his writing has consistently sought to capture the spiritual history of individuals amid shifting social structures. Even in his 2018 novel *The Plain Climber*, he continues to depict the clashes and struggles between urban modernity, contemporary forces, and traditional customs—as well as the eventual defeat of outdated ideologies and ways of life.

It is undeniable that, with the progression of the era and urbanization—especially with the rise of post-60s (1960s-born) and post-70s (1970s-born)

---

① In 2018, *The Sheep's Gate* was finally vindicated—named one of "40 Most Influential Novels of the Reform Era", a long-overdue recognition of Li's legacy.

writers, as well as younger generations of authors—their writing has incorporated more modern and urban elements, reflecting shifts in their upbringing and living environments. As seen in Shao Li's *Minghui's Christmas*, which depicts a woman losing herself in hedonistic excesses, only to rediscover her identity before ultimately achieving tragic self-awakening. Similarly, Qiao Ye's *Demolition Chronicles* portrays the urban-rural fringe during rapid urbanization—where displaced residents exhibit not nostalgia for lost homes, but rather unrestrained human desires. These texts transcend mere realist documentation of society, delving instead into the depths of human nature during this process. They reflect the disorientation and self-rediscovery characteristic of transitional eras, while underscoring the possibility and necessity of reconstructing spiritual worlds. Xi Tongfa's *Sparrow Dialogue* examines the psychological oppression lurking beneath the seemingly glamorous lives of urban youth, simultaneously attempting to explore multiple perspectives for observing the city. Nan Feiyan's *Scorpio* dissects the survival, romantic entanglements, and career struggles of urban civil servants through a seemingly placid narrative, laying bare their existential and developmental histories.

In the contemporary era of burgeoning literary vitality, literature has cast off the dogmatic constraints of the past, growing increasingly diverse and robust—a transformation equally true for writers of the Central Plains region. They have cultivated and experimented within their familiar domains: Shao Li's Temporary Posting Series conducts profound investigations into grassroots cadres' lives with incisive portrayals; Jiao Shu's Mayor Series, drawing from personal secondment experiences, dissects the bureaucratic ecosystem; and Qiao Ye's *Confession* employs narrative implantation to interrogate human nature's complexities amidst historical and contemporary turbulence. It can be said that alongside societal development and deepening diversification, literary subject matter has become increasingly fluid and dynamic. Many writers, through their observations of contemporary society, seek points of convergence between the individual and the era—striving through their craft to engage with and respond to the challenges of real-world China. Yet realist narrative remains the lifeblood of contemporary Chinese literature, with many writers quietly devoting their creative practice to this tradition. Take, for instance, the small-town youths in Zhang Yuntao's works—their restless youth, their lingering attachments, even the trajectories of their lives are rendered with unflinching authenticity across numerous texts. From his writings, we observe that today's rural and small-town youth are no longer the silent generation of the past—they now possess their own vitality and an upwardly mobile force.

Yet the fundamental challenge persists: how should writers apprehend and intervene in reality? With the overwhelming proliferation of social information, some authors, like Yan Lianke, lamented that "reality has grown more absurd than fiction". Certain works are even derided as "compilations of news anecdotes" (e.g., Yu Hua's *The Seventh Day*). Such critiques have engendered profound creative dilemmas, rendering the solemn writer's dual task of societal reflection and realistic representation a pervasive predicament.

In *The Great Tradition*, F.R. Leavis characterized writers acutely attuned to their era as "vanguards of the age"—those who "achieve prescient awareness when the pressures of shifting spiritual atmospheres first register in the most lucid minds." To a significant degree, intellectual acuity should serve as a crucial metric in evaluating writers. Faced with the same realities and narratives, the depth of their critical reflection—even the prescience of their thematic choices—becomes paramount. This compels writers not merely to depict society, but to observe with analytical rigor and interrogate with sustained depth, continuously assessing trajectories amid flux. A transforming society thus imposes escalating demands on literary practice.

In an era of ubiquitous information access and homogenized lived experiences, a writer's ability to channel individualized narratives and deploy singular imagination has become pivotal in determining a work's significance. Within this context, successive generations of writers have cultivated distinctive literary articulations of Henan's urban cultural essence, offering unique epistemological and aesthetic contributions. The essential quality of Henan lies in its immemorial civilizational history. A visit to the ancient exhibitions of the National Museum reveals what amounts to a condensed chronicle of Chinese civilization, whose material narrative unfolds from Shang dynasty bronzes onward, these ritual vessels inaugurating the very codification of Central Plains culture as the root of Huaxia civilization. Through literature, this cultural and geographic legacy not only persists but acquires vitality and singularity. The sedimented history and Central Plains culture remain enshrined in collective memory—from the Yinxu ruins in Anyang and Kaifeng's layered "cities beneath cities," to the recently cinematic-popularized Luoyang spade and tomb-robbing captains, all emerging from this cultural heartland. The seminal anthology *Kaifeng: Urban Imagination and Cultural Memory*, edited by David Der-wei Wang and Guan Aihe, has profoundly shaped scholarship through its investigations of the city's flood folklore, character archetypes, festive rituals, monastic landscapes, and Henan opera traditions. Expanding literary subject matter, the novel form offers broader contextual possibilities. Such attempts not only unlock multidimensional historical perspectives, but also exhibit Henan's distinctive cultural geography and landscapes with remarkable singularity. It can be argued that unlocking Henan's regional cultural dimensions to expand literature's representational scope constitutes a vital marker of a work's distinctiveness—an imperative demanding writers' sustained attention.

The relationship between regional specificity and literary creation has long been a focus of scholarly inquiry. From Hippolyte Taine's tripartite framework of race, milieu, and moment in *The Philosophy of Art* to Mike Crang's *Cultural Geography*—which asserts that "geographical landscapes should not be reduced to physical topography, but rather decoded as legible 'texts'". In classical Chinese literature, movements like the Gong'an School and Tongcheng School, along with modern literary traditions such as Beijing-Style and Shanghai-Style, have all emphasized the isomorphic relationship between regional culture and literary production. Although such research experienced interruptions post-1949, the cultural fever of the 1980s revived fervent explorations of ethnic and regional cultural roots—a pursuit that remains emblematic of contemporary intellectual currents. The city is not merely a site of modernization—it also carries cultural afterlives of profound antiquity and confronts the spiritual imperative to "wait for the soul to catch up". For Henan's urban literature, the critical challenge lies in mining its ancient historical and cultural reservoirs while interrogating the emergent dynamics of modern cities. By synthesizing regional literary traditions with the holistic development of Central Plains urbanity—its interplay of place and people—writers must forge linguistic systems and expressive modes that articulate local sensibilities both materially and affectively, ultimately establishing aesthetic principles with a distinct provincial signature. This dual excavation and innovation constitutes our foremost reading expectation.

www.ingramcontent.com/pod-product-compliance
Lightning Source LLC
LaVergne TN
LVHW010651110826
845149LV00014B/3026

* 9 7 8 1 9 6 5 8 9 0 9 2 9 *